Praise for

Fallen Volume Four

Author Tiffany Aaron definitely caught me off guard
and I applaud her for it. ~ *Jeep Diva*

I0542383

Totally Bound Publishing books by Tiffany Aaron:

Fallen Volume One
Detroit
Reno

Fallen Volume Two
New Orleans
Chicago

Fallen Volume Three
New York
Los Angeles

Fallen Volume Four
London
Saint Petersburg

FALLEN
Volume Four

London

Saint Petersburg

TIFFANY AARON

Fallen Volume Four
ISBN # 978-1-78430-124-8
©Copyright Tiffany Aaron 2014
Cover Art by Posh Gosh ©Copyright 2014
Interior text design by Claire Siemaszkiewicz
Totally Bound Publishing

Published in 2014 by Totally Bound Publishing, Newland House, The Point, Weaver Road, Lincoln, LN6 3QN, United Kingdom.

Totally Bound Publishing is an imprint of Total-E-Ntwined Limited.

LONDON

Dedication

For everyone who hoped Mika'il would have his own
happy ending.

Chapter One

Mika'il stood on top of the Elizabeth Tower, what most people affectionately called Big Ben. He stared out across the London skyline. It had been centuries since he'd been there last. It might have seemed odd that the head archangel had avoided one certain city in the world, but he had because of the memories strolling the streets.

The ghosts of times past haunted all the cities where mortals lived, but the ones bothering Mika'il were personal. He shoved his hands in the pockets of his pants and continued to study the buildings all around him. Yet he wasn't seeing the modern, bustling twenty-first century London. No. He saw the city as it had looked two hundred years earlier when the ton had ruled society with vicious gossip, power and money.

"It's hard to stand here and not see all that has gone on before," Lucifer spoke beside him.

He'd known the fallen was there, had sensed him the moment he had appeared. Yet he wasn't given to worrying about Lucifer right then. He was thinking about another fallen and wondering if she still lived in London, or whether her own private demons had driven her away from the city she adored?

"Such deep thoughts, my friend." Lucifer moved to stand on the very edge of the tower's cupola. "Why are you here? I've never once in close to three hundred years felt your presence in this city. Why come now?"

Taking a deep breath, Mika'il shook off the melancholy threatening to overtake him. "I'm here because Dominic is opening a new club and I want to wish him well on his venture."

"Hmmm..." Lucifer didn't believe him, if Mika'il read the nuance of his tone right.

"What are you doing here, Lucifer? I thought you'd be somewhere else, wreaking havoc and causing trouble. Shouldn't you be anywhere there is strife in the world?" Mika'il raised his eyebrows at Lucifer's cheeky grin.

"Oh but there is strife and conflict everywhere in the world." Lucifer waved his hand at the busy streets below them. "Why should I deny myself the comforts of good food and gorgeous women to go to some Third World country when they can kill themselves easily enough without me around?"

As much as Mika'il wished to argue, he couldn't. Lucifer was right about how mortals were perfectly capable of causing their own troubles without Lucifer egging them on. He faced Lucifer and was stunned at how tired the fallen angel seemed.

Lucifer was paler than usual, and his cheeks were sunken, almost as though he hadn't been eating, which worried Mika'il. Angels didn't need to eat and Lucifer shouldn't look like he was starving.

"Are you okay?" He took a step toward Lucifer.

"What? Are you actually showing concern, Mika'il? How would the Father feel about that? You're supposed to ignore me and not worry your pretty little head about what I do." Lucifer dismissed his question with sarcasm. "I'm fine. Just tired of being surrounded by these mortals who blame all their shit on me instead of taking responsibility for their own actions."

Mika'il winced at the bitterness in the other angel's tone, which seemed strong this time — as if Lucifer had become less tolerant of mortal foibles. Yet why would Lucifer lose patience with the evil men did to each other when he gained from it?

"Go have fun with your friends, Mika'il. Don't waste time wondering about me. I'll be fine. I always am." Lucifer bowed slightly before he disappeared in a shimmer of power.

"*Mika'il, are you coming?*" Dominic LaFontaine, the Enforcer whose club Mika'il had come to visit, asked.

"*I'll be there in a few minutes. I have something to do first. Don't hold anything up for my sake.*"

"*Certainly. We'll see you when you get here.*"

There was no questioning or curiosity in Dominic's voice and Mika'il realized that no one would ask him about his actions. Well, no one except for Lucifer, and usually that was only because Lucifer knew it annoyed Mika'il when he asked.

Heaving a silent sigh, Mika'il focused his mind on an estate in Northumberland. He closed his eyes and gathered his power, letting it wash over him. The next time he opened his eyes, he found himself standing in the front yard of a large stone house.

Looking around, Mika'il didn't see anyone, so he strolled toward the entrance of the building and sadness drifted through him. When he'd last been here, two hundred years ago, the asylum had been newly built and the grounds well maintained.

Now the stones had tumbled down and it was in ruins. Nature was reclaiming the area, but in Mika'il's mind, he saw it the way it used to look. He wandered into what would have been the foyer of the building. Standing in the middle of the entrance, he turned slowly in a circle, seeing the grandeur in the faded, broken walls.

He thought about going up the sweeping staircase to his room, but it didn't look very sturdy. While falling through it wouldn't kill him, it would hurt and he didn't want to have to deal with that. He decided to make his way to the gardens in the back. That was the place that had really touched his heart and made sure that he'd never forget his time there.

Winding his way through the ruins of the estate, he saw flashes of spirits as they appeared then disappeared. Mika'il ignored them as he continued to the wide French doors that led out into the gardens behind the mansion. Amazement washed through him when he saw that the doors were still intact and all the glass as well. Aside from faded paint, the doors looked just the same.

Mika'il almost glanced around to see where the other patients were, but caught himself because there wasn't anyone there. Taking a deep breath, he pushed open the door then stepped out.

The gardens were overgrown, but he could still see the paths he used to wander with Bridget. As soon as he thought of her, he smiled. There had been sunshine in her laughter and it was something he'd never believed he would find in a place like the hospital had been back then.

"Mika'il, where are you?" Celeste's voice came through his memories.

"I'll be there in a few minutes," he told her and strolled out toward a small clearing.

"All right." Again there were no more questions or digging into what he was doing.

Where had Bridget gone after she'd left the asylum? He'd checked on her, but for some reason, he hadn't been able to find her again. He'd asked God to tell him where Bridget had gone, and had been shocked when God had told him he couldn't.

After searching for over a year and not being able to discover where the woman he'd fallen in love with had gone, Mika'il had vowed never to return to England. It hurt too much to think about her being out in the world without him.

He slammed the door in his mind shut on those thoughts and memories. It wasn't time for him to revisit them. He doubted he would ever want to think about what he'd been through and what he'd lost during those years. Yet maybe he would come back to look around some more after he'd met with the Enforcers and their lovers.

His power swirled around and in him as he gathered it then let it go, shimmering out of view from the garden. When his power dissipated, he found himself standing in Soho in front of a building that looked as though it was still under renovations.

"I'm here," he sent a thought to Dominic.

A minute later, the door opened and a mortal gestured for him to come in. "Be careful of the flooring. We're just finishing it up. Mr LaFontaine said you can join them in the VIP area."

"Thank you." He nodded to the man as he walked past, winding his way through the workers.

"Mika'il, where have you been?" Danielle called as he approached where they all sat.

"Playing tourist, no doubt," William joked. "That's what Abby and I are going to do the next couple of days until the club opens."

"The city has changed since I was here last," Mika'il commented.

He gave each of the ladies a kiss on the cheek and shook hands with the men. Then he unbuttoned his suit coat before sitting in the booth.

Teresa smiled at him. "When was the last time you came to London?"

"I left England in eighteen hundred and sixteen, shortly after the end of the Napoleonic Wars."

"You haven't been back in just under two hundred years. Why? I would think you would come back here as often as you could." Christian waved his hand toward the front of the club. "I love this city almost as much as I love New York."

Mika'il shrugged. "There are millions of cities and countries out there for me to check in on. I don't like coming back here."

"You don't like to come here?" William asked as he narrowed his eyes to look at Mika'il.

Sighing, Mika'il wished he hadn't said that. Of all the things he didn't really want to talk about, his not liking London was near the top of the list. "Yes, I don't like coming to England. Dominic, are you on schedule to open Fallen Angel Deux on time?"

He was pretty sure that Dominic would've rather pursued the other conversation, but he must have seen something in Mika'il's eyes that warned him against it. "Yes. I'd be very upset if they fell behind at this point in the process."

"I told you O'Leary was the best construction company I knew of here in London," Adam spoke up.

Mika'il turned to look at Adam Montgomery, Celeste's mortal husband. "Is he one of your unsavory connections?"

"Excuse me, since falling in love with a certain fallen angel, I no longer have unsavory connections." Adam glanced at the people surrounding him. "Except for this bunch."

Dominic and William protested while Christian sat next to Mika'il then leaned closer to him.

"What's wrong?"

"What do you mean?" He could hedge with the best of them.

Christian frowned. "I know you far better than the others. They won't question you too closely, but I have no problem doing so."

He'd forgotten that Christian didn't feel the need to respect his privacy. "Sticking your nose into my business?"

"Why not, when you do it to us all the time? Don't think I haven't figured out what you've done."

"What have I done?" Mika'il tried to look innocent, but he must not have got it right.

"After talking to all of these couples, I came to realize you did your best to get us together. Why was it so important for us to be with these particular mortals? You talked to each of them during the time we were falling in love." Christian reached out to touch Joan's hand. "I thank you for pushing us together, but why?"

Mika'il noticed the silence and he saw that the others were staring at them. He hadn't been given permission to tell them, so there wasn't much he could say. "All I can say is you were all meant to be together. That is why you found each other how and when you did. You helped and gave up something for each other."

Danielle laughed. "I'm not sure I gave up anything for Grant."

"Yes, you did. You gave up your secrets. You'd spent centuries never telling anyone who you were, yet you told Grant." Mika'il smiled. "Sure, it was because he found something he shouldn't have."

"You made sure he'd discover it and have to ask my help to figure out what it was," Danielle pointed out. "He never would've dug up Ferguson's body if you hadn't pointed him in the right direction."

"I was following orders. The Father doesn't tell me everything. I do what I'm told." He shifted in his seat, not liking the fact that he didn't seem to have control of the situation.

"So tell us why you don't like coming to London?" Grant enquired.

Mika'il shook his head. "It's none of your business. You know, I do have other things to do besides watching over Enforcers and fallens. The reason I don't like it here has nothing to do with any of you."

"Of course it doesn't," Christian said. "I haven't lived in England since I moved to New York during the colonial times. I don't think any of you have been here lately, have you? Aside from Dominic, of course."

He took a deep breath as he thought about everything that had happened to him while he'd lived in England all those long years ago. Would they understand why he'd done what he had? Would they think he was crazy for asking to become mortal for a little while?

"I used to live here during the eighteen hundreds."

William frowned. "Lived here? I didn't think you lived anywhere except Heaven or that waiting room of yours."

"There was a time where I wanted to get to know mortals better. I felt like I was losing my compassion for them, so I asked God to make me human." Mika'il ran his fingers over the surface of the table.

Silence fell like rocks into the river of noise that had been bubbling around them. The shock wave rippled out until even the construction workers quietened slightly. Mika'il took a deep breath then looked up to see all of the fallen and their lovers staring at him.

"Why the hell would you ask God that?" Christian looked stunned as he waved his hand to encompass the fallen. "We've spent centuries hating what our reckless choices have made us, and you casually ask the Father to make you mortal. Did you hit your head or something?"

His comment broke the wall of shock and the others started chattering at Mika'il about it as well. Finally, it was Abby who held up her hand to stop them as Mika'il contemplated leaving.

"This is probably why he never spoke of it to you," she pointed out. "He knew you'd all lose your minds."

"But, Abby love, you don't understand," William protested. "Those of us who rebelled have always been looking for a way to become what we once were. Yet he willingly gave up his angelic powers to be mortal. What kind of idiot does that?"

"Obviously he didn't give them up. He's still an archangel and wields more power than we can even imagine." Celeste said as she shook her head. "You must have had a reason why you did it."

"I told you. I was losing my compassion for mortals. I watched as they did all these horrible things to each other, and I couldn't blame it all on Lucifer either. He's insane or close to it, but he can't be everything at once." Mika'il fidgeted with the glass of whiskey one of the waiters had brought over. "I wanted to see what they go through every day and why they act like they do."

"And God did this?" Grant sounded skeptical. "I wouldn't think he'd do something like that. Not with you. I mean you're the warrior angel. You're *the* archangel."

"No, I'm not *the* archangel. There are others just as important as I am." Mika'il didn't ever want anyone to think he was so important that he was irreplaceable. "When I was gone, you didn't notice a difference, did you?"

There was a momentary pause while they thought back to that time. He knew there hadn't been any big issues that had come up while he'd been mortal, because God would've brought him back to take care of them. It wasn't as though he had wanted to be mortal for the rest of eternity—Mika'il had simply wanted to find a reason to care about humans instead of becoming like Lucifer, and finding them too insignificant to love.

"You know what? I do remember wondering where you were, but not being overly concerned that I couldn't get a hold of you. Nothing happened that I couldn't deal with." Dominic relaxed back into the cushions of the booth. "But what does you having been mortal have to do with you not liking England?"

"It has everything to do with me not liking this place," he muttered, not really wanting to go into detail, but knowing now that he'd opened that particular can of worms, they would worry at it like a dog with a bone. He was mixing his clichés and metaphors, but he didn't care.

"Was there a woman involved?" Teresa enquired softly and her perception amazed him.

He shot her a quick glance. "What makes you ask that?"

"There's always a woman involved in these situations," she said with a wink, showing Mika'il that she was only half joking. "Is she the reason why you haven't returned here?"

He swallowed and thought, knowing that what he said next could change how they all saw him. He would no longer be the infallible Mika'il, the angel who kept himself high above the fray of love, lust and humanness. Mika'il had found himself caught up in the very things he disdained as an angel.

"I spent two years here in London, moving amongst the ton and the poor. I tried to find what made them so fascinating to the Father. I tried to remember why I needed to show them compassion and love. I couldn't begin to understand why they did what they did to each other. Then I was committed to an asylum in the north. It was there I discovered something that broke my heart and gave me back the very empathy I'd lost." Closing his eyes, Mika'il brought Bridget's face up in his memories and he sighed.

"What was it? Or should I be asking who it was?" Joan was sitting next to him and he felt her bump her shoulder against his.

"I met an angel who didn't know she was one, and she broke my heart with her struggles against her memories of Heaven. Unfortunately, she had no idea what those memories meant." Mika'il opened his eyes to see all of them staring at him again. "I fell in love with her then lost her when I returned to Heaven."

Chapter Two

Bridget crouched in the doorway, unsure of where exactly she was. Sometimes her mind wandered and she ended up places in the city she'd never been before. Those episodes made it quite difficult to get back to Regent's Park.

"Come on, lady. You can't sit there."

She looked up into the expressionless face of a police officer. Shrinking away from his touch, Bridget rocketed to her feet.

"I'm going. I'm going," she muttered, shuffling in the direction of the closest Tube station, or at least what she thought was the right direction. She spotted the Marble Arch and knew there had to be a station nearby.

"Bridget, think about it, my dear girl. You have your Oyster card and you know which line is for the park. It's not hard." The same voice she'd been hearing since she could first remember spoke to her.

"I know, but it *is* hard," she mumbled, well aware of how she looked and smelled by the way the people avoided getting close to her.

Dirt encrusted jeans and a faded, torn T-shirt were all she wore against the rain she could feel was about to start. Her tennis shoes had holes in the soles, and even though she'd lined them with cardboard, her feet would still get wet.

She needed to be back in her place before the storm rolled in. Bridget couldn't get caught in the open — not after having spent two days in Northwick Park Hospital in Harrow after her last break with reality.

Bridget had to admit that at least while she'd been in hospital, she'd had a warm bed and food to eat. Yet she hated how the nurses had stared at her as though she really was crazy.

"I'm not crazy," she mumbled as she tapped her card to the machine. "Doesn't matter what any doctor says. I know that what I hear and see is real."

"Hey, you bloody cunt, get yer arse outta the way," some man behind her yelled.

She ducked then made her way down the tunnel to the platform. She glanced at the map, almost but not quite touching the lines as she tried to figure out where she had to go.

"I have to take the Central line to Oxford Circus. I get off there and switch to the Bakerloo line that will take me to Regent's Park. From there I can make my way back to my spot without getting into any trouble."

Having a plan made her feel better because not having one caused her a great deal of stress when she couldn't decide which way to go or where she needed to be. It didn't help when her visions took over her reality and she couldn't tell the difference between them. When that happened, she would find herself curled up in an out of the way spot, muttering to herself in some language she'd never spoken before.

Thunderstorms were the worst for her. It was as though she was having flashbacks, but as far as she knew she'd never been in a war or any other kind of traumatic situation. Of course, that didn't seem to matter. Had there been something in her past that she'd forgotten? Something that had caused her to blank out whole parts of her life?

"Bridget, you know the solution can't be that easy. Your memories go back farther than this life. You've been alive since the world began, or so it must feel sometimes."

She sighed. "I know, but can't I choose to believe I'm normal? That I'm not schizophrenic like the doctors have labeled me. Don't I have the right to live like other mortals?"

"If you were mortal, you would certainly deserve it, but you know the truth. It has been inside of you for centuries, and you discovered it when you met Myles."

Smiling, she let her mind wander to the moment she'd laid eyes on Myles at the asylum in Northumberland. He'd looked at her and it was almost like his silver eyes had seen into her soul and understood her pain.

"He was wonderful, Lucercio," she said as she settled into a seat on the Tube. She'd made sure to keep her head down, though she knew people watched her. Usually their stares held pity or disgust, or a mixture of both emotions. Rarely were there any who had sympathy or understanding for her in their eyes.

When she ran into someone who was sympathetic, she wanted to say something to them, but she couldn't bring herself to. What if she was wrong? What if she was only seeing what she wanted to see in their eyes?

Lucercio snorted and she heard his frustration in the sound.

"But see there's the thing. You're not real either," she pointed out, glancing up to make sure she hadn't missed her stop. "Bond Street. I have one more stop before Oxford Circus."

"That's right, and I'm as real as you are. You've seen me before," Lucercio pointed out.

"How do I know you were real and not one of my visions? That's the problem with them. I can't tell which visions are visions and which images are real." She curled into herself as the car became more and more crowded.

No one wanted to sit or stand near her and she got why they wouldn't, but there wasn't anything she could do about it. It was hard to keep clean when she spent her days and nights on the streets, avoiding being a victim herself.

None of the commuters acknowledged her and Bridget liked it that way. She liked to pass unnoticed among the people who called London their home. She'd watched it grow from a Roman outpost in a hostile country to the vibrant bustling city it was now. She'd never strayed far from its borders, except when she'd been committed to the place in Northumberland. But other than that, she'd always called London sanctuary from the nightmares haunting her.

"I'm real, my dear girl, and someday soon, you'll finally discover your true soul. Now you must get off at Oxford Circus, then take the Bakerloo line to Regent's Park stop."

"I know that. I'd already figured it out." Bridget fingered her card and a small piece of paper in her pocket. Frowning, she pulled it out.

The paper was stained with jagged edges and the ink was faded, yet she could make out the words.

The tears of an angel hold the memories of a thousand broken hearts and the dreams of a million hopeful souls.

The strong handwriting definitely wasn't hers and the old-fashioned spelling said it had come from a different generation. Hell, maybe even a different century. She rubbed her thumb over the stylized 'M' at the bottom of the note.

"Myles," she whispered, tears welling though she fought against them.

Two hundred years ago, he'd been standing in the middle of the hedge maze on the asylum's estate, staring up at the sky as though he was pleading with someone—or something—for what? She didn't know and hadn't wanted to interrupt him, so she'd turned to go back the way she'd come, but her foot had landed on a dry leaf. The crunch of it falling apart under her foot had drawn his attention from his contemplation of the heavens.

She'd frozen under his sterling silver gaze and his smile had spoken to her on the deepest levels possible. If Bridget was ever to love someone, it would've been Myles who'd peered into her soul, seen all the shattered bits and decided that it was worth gluing all her broken pieces back together.

For five months, he had been her constant companion, when they could be together. He had talked to her about her visions and the voices she heard. He'd never judged her because he had been sent there for the same reason. Maybe it was because he understood what it was like to have no one believe him, or even try to help, when things were at their worst.

Bridget heard the voice announce "Oxford Circus" and she shoved the note in her pocket before standing to push her way through the crowded car to the door. A woman in a tailored business suit sneered at her.

"Where does someone like you come up with the money for an Underground pass?"

"How does a woman like you come up with the money for that ridiculously expensive suit?" Bridget asked.

"I earned it," the woman said and condemnation dripped from her voice.

Bridget nodded. "Well, I earned the money for this, as well as for a three bedroom flat in Soho, honey. Don't judge a book by its cover."

She snorted. "Right. I'm supposed to believe that."

"Believe it or not. It's no skin off my nose either way." Bridget stepped from the car as the doors opened. She ignored the flow of people in all directions while making her way to the Bakerloo platform.

That was another thing that bothered her more than anything else. Yes, she looked homeless and there were nights and days where she didn't go back to her flat because her mind, so fractured with memories and illusions, led her down dark paths and through shadowy parts of the city. That didn't mean she couldn't afford to pay rent or didn't in some way contribute to society.

There was a reason for her existence. She had to believe that, or she'd lose her tenuous grip on the demented reality she lived. Myles had held her at times when she'd gone under the swelling wave of panic and loss, whispering in her ear that she was meant to hold on until it was time for her to return home.

She arrived on the platform just as the train showed up, so she strolled onto the car like she owned it.

"Fuck them all who believe that I shouldn't be treated like a human just because I wear dirty clothes and my hair isn't brushed."

Glaring around, Bridget cleared out a space so she didn't have to worry about anyone invading it. Of course, smelling like she did probably helped more than her attitude.

"Good girl. You need to deal with your woe is me attitude. It makes you a victim and you, my dear, aren't one. You are subjected to pressures outside anyone's realm of understanding and I think you are stronger for it."

"Like a piece of coal being pressed into a diamond," she commented out loud, not caring if the people stared at her. Most of them probably thought she was talking on a Bluetooth anyway.

"Exactly that. Now I must go. Get back to your flat before the storm starts. There might be something waiting for you there."

With that cryptic message, Lucercio's presence was gone from her head and Bridget felt as though she could think for herself again. There were moments when he seemed to almost take up all her brain and she couldn't function at full capacity with him in there.

Exhaling, she released the tension from her shoulders and back. A throb set up behind her eyes, making her happy that she was on her way home because a migraine was starting, something that usually happened after one of her episodes.

"Regent's Park," the announcer said over the loudspeaker.

"Not far now," she informed herself. "You can go home and pass out for a while. Hopefully, you won't do anything stupid while you're sleeping."

After making her way two blocks from the park to her flat, she dug her keys out of her pockets then let herself in. She locked the door behind her then dropped to the floor. Curling into a ball, she wrapped her arms around her stomach and whispered a prayer as a vision swept over her.

She stood on a plain created of white sand, or at least she thought it was sand. It was hard to tell and she didn't have time to reach down to touch it. Holding a sword in one hand, she carried a shield with the other.

"Bridget, watch out," someone called to her and she turned just in time to spot another sword coming down at her.

Bridget blocked it with her shield then drove her blade into her attacker's side. The gasp of his hot breath over her cheek caught her off guard, then he dissolved in front of her to be replaced by another soldier and another. Each time she killed one, another took his place.

There was no end to the carnage. She lost her shield and the blood kept causing her hand to slip on the grip of her sword. There had to be cuts on almost every part of her body because she knew it wasn't just her opponents' blood that covered her.

When there seemed to be a break in the fighting, she bent over to brace her hands on her knees, breathing hard while trying to get a hold on the pain threatening to overtake her.

"Bridget, are you all right?"

As she glanced up, the sight greeting her wasn't one she was used to in this particular battle. A distinguished man, mid to late fifties, stood next her. He wore a tailored black pin-striped suit with a snazzy red velvet vest under the jacket.

A soldier raced up behind him, raising his sword while running.

"Watch out," she cried, pushing the man aside before swinging her weapon in a downward arch. The jolt of it hitting his flesh ricocheted through her. "You shouldn't be here."

"Bridget, stop. You're having an episode. What you're seeing isn't real." He put his hands on her face, bringing her gaze up to his. Worried brown eyes met hers. "I'm Russell. Remember me?"

She blinked. The name sounded familiar and it tried to fight its way through her troubled brain. Shaking her head, Bridget looked around her to see the strangest scene. There were soldiers in white battling soldiers in red in the middle of her flat. How was that possible?

"Bridget Langston, do you remember me? I'm Russell Walvoski, your friend." He patted her cheeks with his soft hands. "Come on. You were doing so well there, even with your little disappearing act the other night."

"Disappearing act?" She ducked as another enemy tried to stab her, but when there wasn't any pain, she shook her head again. Everything disappeared around her except for her flat and the man standing in front of her.

"Russell?" Tears filled her eyes. "Did I have an episode? How did you get in here?"

"I have a key, honey. Remember you gave it to me after the last episode. When we had to break the door down because no one could get a hold of you. We needed to have a fail safe way to keep you here in this reality with us." There was a flash of red in his eyes then they returned to the gentle brown she remembered.

Swallowing, Bridget clicked her tongue against her teeth as she cleaned her mind of all that had just happened. "You're right. I gave you the key so you could come check on me in case I don't answer the phone or the door. It's because I have these episodes."

Russell stepped back then took her hand. She had climbed to her feet at some point during the vision but she didn't know when or how. As he led her to a chair, her knees trembled and her body ached as though she'd been in a real fight.

"Sit. I'll make us some tea. Have you eaten yet?" At her shrug, he chuckled a little. "All right then. We'll have a proper tea with biscuits, scones and sandwiches. If you have all the stuff I need."

"How long was I gone this time?"

He shot a quick glance over his shoulder at her while he strolled to her kitchen area. Her flat was actually a large loft, taking up the entire top floor of one of the buildings. She had a big butcher's block island and state-of-the-art appliances. Russell had been in her place enough to know where everything was, so she drew her feet up to rest them on the edge of the chair then laid her cheek on her knees.

"Hmm... Today is Wednesday and the last I talked to you was on Saturday, so you've been wandering for four days. I had already talked to the police to go looking for you, though I really am glad you're back without involving them completely." He hummed softly while he went through the calming ritual of making tea and the little snacks they would be enjoying with it.

"I'm sorry," she whispered, tears trickling down her cheeks. "I don't know why this happens."

"Ah, honey, it's all right. I know you don't mean for them to happen, but they do and until we figure out why, we deal with the outcome. Now why don't you go take a warm shower, clean up, and change into some warm clothes? Once I'm done here, I'll call off the law."

She pushed to her feet, pausing for a few seconds to make sure she could move without falling down. Once she'd found her balance, she wandered over to brush a kiss over Russell's cheek then went to where her bed and dresser were sectioned off from the rest of the living space by tri-fold Chinese silk screens. Bridget dug out a pair of flannel pajama pants and a fleece sweatshirt. She also grabbed a pair of fuzzy socks. Even though it wasn't particularly cold at that time in London, it was rainy and she got chilled easily after one of her flights of fancy, as Russell called them.

Chapter Three

In the club, the fallen stared at Mika'il and he didn't want to meet any of their gazes.

"You were in love with a girl?"

He glared at William. "You don't have to sound so shocked. I can appreciate a beautiful woman."

"It's not that. I think it's almost like realizing our parents had sex," Abby suggested while poking William with her elbow.

"The thing is, I thought angels weren't supposed to fall in love with mortals. I thought you were supposed to be celibate and all that crap," Grant murmured.

"We are if we aren't fallen," Christian informed them while he stared at Mika'il. "But something tells me the rules didn't apply here."

"I wasn't an angel. I was mortal in every way except for my memories. I remembered being in Heaven and dealing with angels. I couldn't forget the Fall, no matter how much I wanted to at that time." Mika'il went back to studying the table, not wanting them to stare at him like he was some unusual bug they'd just come across.

Danielle nudged him. "What happened?"

"Don't you all have something better to do than to relive the past with me?"

"Not if that past makes you look so sad." Joan touched his hand. "You look as sad as Lucifer did when I talked to him."

Great. Now I'm being compared to him. Mika'il cleared his throat. "All right. It was around eighteen hundred and ten when I went to God and asked him to make me mortal. I didn't care how long it would be. I needed to find my compassion for these humans that he loved. I lost so many emotions dealing with them over the millennia I worked with them. As they evolved, things got worse. I wanted to know what it was like being human."

"And the Father did it? I'm sorry, but I don't get why he'd allow his chief archangel to leave Heaven." Dominic frowned.

Mika'il chuckled. "He wasn't worried about me being gone. It's not like God can't deal with the problems on his own. I guess he understood why I wanted to do it and he loves humans more than anything in the world. Why wouldn't he want me to feel that same kind of love?"

"So God makes you mortal. Then what happens?" Celeste asked.

Mika'il stood up while some settled into their seats, others leaning forward, and he saw the eagerness on their faces. Of course they were eager. They'd never thought he would be subject to the same feelings and thoughts they had. He had become almost God-like in their eyes, though he would never think that of himself.

He turned away from them to look out of one of the uncovered windows at the cars and people passing by outside. As he watched, the scenery changed. Instead of cars, there were horse-drawn carriages being driven past, and the people weren't dressed in jeans. Mika'il smiled as he watched a man tip his hat to a lady who nodded back at him before sweeping past.

"I decided to come to London. It was one of the busiest cities in the world and teeming with mortals. I thought if there was one place I could learn how to be human, it was here." He gestured at the city beyond the window. "I appeared out of nowhere, but I had money and charm. I'd made sure to have some, not wanting to be left high and dry."

"You didn't get the experience of the average mortal who has to work every day for money?" Adam enquired.

"Maybe not, but I wandered the streets from the East End to Grosvenor Square. I watched how they interacted with each other. What they talked about and how they loved. I was like a child free from the nursery for the first time and exploring the enormous world I'd found outside the doors." He stuffed his hands in his pockets before he started to pace.

"What went wrong? How did you meet this amazing woman you haven't been able to forget in two hundred years?" Grant urged him on in his story.

"I tried to fit in and become an accepted member of the ton. Yet for some reason known only to him, when God made me mortal, he allowed me to retain my memories of what I used to be. It was difficult to deal with and I made the mistake of talking about it to someone. Just like that, my eccentricities weren't tolerated because they were the ramblings of a crazy person."

Mika'il clenched his hands and stifled his snarl. He'd seen the worst in people when that had happened.

How they'd turned on him because he'd been perceived as different or strange. "My so-called friends had me committed, which I hadn't realized they could do without a family member or something. But somehow they convinced the staff at the asylum that I was a danger to the public."

"That's horrible." Teresa gasped and he shot her a glance to see that she'd covered her mouth with her hand and tears gleamed in her eyes.

He nodded. "It was. There were no laws governing mental hospitals back then, and not a lot of understanding about mental illness. Patients were subjected to terrible treatments and experiments all in the name of science and medical advancement."

Mika'il paced from one end of the club to the other, no longer concerned or even thinking about the people who sat watching him, or the construction workers who had stopped what they were doing to listen to him. He ignored them as memories of those treatments and experiments wound their way through his head. Somehow he and Bridget had been lucky enough to avoid most of them, but there had been some very unlucky patients who'd borne the brunt of the doctors' disregard. Even after he'd gone back to Heaven, back to being what he had been created to be, he'd still heard their screams and crying.

"It was the hardest thing to listen to them and know I couldn't do anything because I was a mere mortal. A mortal deemed insane and not worthy of anyone's respect," he muttered.

"What about the girl? What was she in there for?"

He didn't know who'd asked the question and he didn't care.

An image of Bridget appeared before him. Her long, blonde curls cascading down her back. Her bright green eyes shining with happiness as she looked up at him. She'd been small, barely reaching his chin, but he'd been able to see the strength in her. There had been a joie de vivre in Bridget that had shocked him because of where they were.

She'd explained how she heard voices and saw visions. None of them made any sense to her, but she'd gotten used to dealing with them. Unfortunately, someone had seen her have an episode and she'd been sent to the asylum.

Mika'il had held her through a couple of those visions and his heart had broken at how wrecked she'd been when she emerged from them.

"She was there for the same reason I was," he said. "She had visions of a life she never could've lived. Of course, she didn't even understand what she was seeing. No one could explain it to her either."

"Not even you?" Joan asked.

"I wasn't an angel anymore. While I still retained my memories, I didn't have any of my powers to look into her mind. I had no way of knowing the truth of what her mind wanted her to know."

He clasped his hands behind his back as he paused in the middle of what was to be the dance floor. He no longer saw the chaos around him.

He stood at the center of the hedge maze on the asylum's grounds, looking up at the sky. His heart yearned for something he barely remembered at the edges of his soul.

A leaf crunched behind him and Mika'il turned to see a petite, dark-blonde woman frozen at the edge of the clearing. Her light hazel eyes gleamed in the sunlight as she watched him. Mika'il simply smiled. Her smile trembled, but it was there, and she took a step toward him.

Bowing, Mika'il introduced himself. "I'm Myles. It's a pleasure to make your acquaintance."

33

It wasn't proper for a single man to talk to a single female without having been introduced first, but manners and rules were lax in a place like this one. Most of the people who lived in the County Asylum of Northumberland weren't ever going to return to the society that had turned their backs on them.

"I'm Bridget." Her lyrical voice was a little husky, as though she'd screamed a lot and her throat ached. She let him take her hand as she curtsied.

He studied her while he drew her over to a stone bench. He gestured for her to sit and was amazed by her graceful form as she spread her dress around her before resting her hands in her lap.

"Why are you here?"

And with that question, their friendship began.

Mika'il came back to the present when a board clattered to the floor from one of the workers' hands. He shook himself and inhaled deeply before he turned to look at his friends. "We spent as much time together as we could every day. The nurses and attendants in Northumberland were quite lenient with us. Maybe because we weren't violent, not even during our worst episodes."

"What were your visions?"

He met Christian's gaze while thinking about Abby's question. *What had they been of?*

"I assume they were of Heaven and angels I'd known before." His jacket tugged on his shoulders as he shrugged. "It's been a long time, plus I've done a lot of things in between. To be honest, Bridget is the only person—or thing—I remember clearly from that time as a mortal."

Teresa rested her head on Dominic's shoulder before she said, "I understand why. The actual experience of being mortal wasn't fun for you, but Bridget wormed her way into your heart. Once you've loved someone, you don't forget them, no matter how long ago it was."

Mika'il was afraid that was true, yet he couldn't help wishing that his memories of Bridget had faded over the centuries. They hadn't—the sound of her laughter and her tears were still razor sharp, cutting into him every time he thought of them.

Giving himself a mental shake, Mika'il looked at Dominic. "Let me know when the grand opening is and I'll come."

It was time to leave. He didn't want to stay there any longer. His heart was glad that his friends were happy and they had found their other halves, but it hurt to watch them.

"Mika'il, we're going to a gallery opening tonight," Joan informed him when he took a step toward the door. "You're welcome to come with us."

While his first reaction was to politely decline, he paused to think about it for a minute. He had nothing pressing that had to be checked out. For the first time in a while, the world was quiet or—at least the fallen were. Oh, there was still fighting and skirmishes going on, but those were situations that were always happening. No matter how much he'd like for them to stop, he couldn't do anything about them right then.

A gentle, warm breeze ruffled his hair and he smiled. "I'd love to join you, Joan. What is the name of the gallery? I'll meet you there."

"It's the Walvoski Gallery on Grafton Street in Mayfair. The show opens at eight." Joan seemed thrilled that he'd agreed to go with them, or maybe she was excited about seeing the art.

"And considering there are six females in this group, we'll probably be there around ten," Grant joked. The females in questions immediately pummeled him and the other men just sat there laughing as he complained.

"You brought it on yourself," William pointed out then he turned to face Mika'il. "Wait. I wanted to ask you. How are Nevan and Cassandra?"

Mika'il sighed. "Nevan's healing quite well, considering how serious his injuries were from the torture. It was still too soon for him to fly, which is why they couldn't come. I'm sure he told you that when you asked, Dominic."

"Yes, and Cassandra doesn't want to leave his side." Dominic stroked the back of his fingers over Teresa's cheek. "I understand how she feels."

"He'll eventually be back to a hundred percent, but it'll take a while. Maybe that's a good thing, because it'll give him and Cassandra time to solidify their relationship." Mika'il glanced at his watch. "I have to go, but I'll see you all tonight."

He wandered from the club out onto the sidewalk. Looking from right to left, he watched as people walked by on their way to work or their homes. *They wander through their lives with no real awareness of what's going on. How would they react if they knew that angels did exist and that there really were monsters in the shadows?*

Most mortals were oblivious to what went on around them and it never surprised him when bad things happened to them. Oh, it didn't make him happy or anything—he didn't wish for any mortal to be hurt. Yet he couldn't help thinking that they should be willing to open their eyes and minds to the possibility of there being other things out in the world.

He turned left before strolling away from Dominic's club. As he went, he gathered his power to him and when he turned the corner, he thought of the white walls of his office. In an instant, he dissolved from the London sidewalk to reappear a second later in front of his desk.

The surface was empty and that made him happy. He wasn't interested in doing paperwork or going through any petitions. After hanging his jacket on a small hook, he unbuttoned his sleeves before rolling them up. He stalked into the garden that stretched out from all sides of his office.

He stuffed his hands in the pockets of his slacks while he wandered along the stone pathways, not really paying attention to which direction he turned until his shoes hit the spongy softness of grass instead of the hard rocks he'd been walking on.

Lifting his head, he glanced around at the clearing. It was a perfect replication of the center of the hedge maze at the asylum. He settled on the stone bench before he let his gaze rest on the fountain in the middle. The marble angel lifted her hands to the sky while her wings were spread out from her back. Water spilled from her eyes in a torrent of crystal liquid as if she were crying. She looked real and if Mika'il had wanted to waste power, he could have made her breathe and move.

He'd done it once when missing Bridget had gotten to be too much to bear. But he knew the statue wasn't real and letting her go back to being stone had hurt as much as letting Bridget go all those years ago.

The garden appeared exactly as he remembered it, yet he knew that if someone else were to come out here, it would look completely different. Nevan called it Limbo, and Mika'il didn't try to explain what it really was.

The Waiting Room, where Mika'il often met recently departed souls, was a holding place and the area surrounding it could be whatever a particular soul wanted. Mika'il and Nevan saw a garden, though he was sure they weren't the same kind. Another soul who arrived would see a beach or even a desert.

It had always been there and the power it held awed Mika'il at times. Some of the angels whispered that it was the fabled Garden of Eden, which had disappeared from Earth once Adam and Eve were banished. None of them knew for sure, and Mika'il had never asked because it didn't matter to him.

He leaned back on his hands, locking his elbows as he looked up into the bright blue sky, wondering where Bridget had gone.

Chapter Four

"Bridget love, you have to do this," Russell pleaded.

She shook her head. "No, I don't. Not really. All those paintings will sell whether I'm there or not. You know most of those people come to see the crazy artist and whisper behind my back." Shoving her hair out of her face, she scowled at her agent. "I hate being put on display like a gorilla in a zoo."

Russell took one of her hands in his then led her to her bedroom area. "I know, honey, and I would do anything to say you could stay home and paint. Hell, I'm loving the canvas you're working on now. I know going to these openings destroys your mojo or creative process or whatever you want to call it. But I let you off the hook last time and you promised you would go to the next one. Well, dear, it's the next one."

Bridget grimaced but didn't protest when Russell handed her a red silk dress. "I did say that, didn't I?"

"Yes, you did and you've never broken a promise to me yet. Don't do it tonight." He went to the armoire set against one of the brick walls. After opening the doors, he bent to dig through her pile of shoes. "Hurry up and get changed. I'll find the heels that go with the dress."

Now that she couldn't argue with him anymore about going, Bridget stripped out of her paint-streaked sweats and T-shirt. She snatched a bra and panties out of the dresser before she raced into the bathroom. She checked her image in the mirror, making sure she didn't have any splotches of paint in her hair. They didn't have enough time for her to wash and blow-dry her mane of curls.

Bridget twisted it up into a bun before stepping under the showerhead. She didn't care that the water was cold. The shock of it helped drag her further away from her creative stupor. When her muse was on her, she rarely stopped long enough to eat, much less take showers or change her clothes. So more often than not, she ended up looking homeless even while in the privacy of her own flat.

She quickly shaved, making sure that everything was smooth and neat before she shut off the water. Stepping onto the bathmat, Bridget called to Russell, "Is anyone important going to be there?"

"They're all important," Russell yelled back and she heard a thump as he must have shut the armoire doors.

"Are some more important than others? Who do I need to suck up to, to get them to buy my outrageously priced paintings?"

Bridget toweled down before dressing as fast as she could. Minimum makeup highlighted her hazel eyes and plump lips. She let her hair down then fluffed it a little, the curls springing off her fingers.

"Come on, Bridget. You look lovely as always. The car will be here any minute now." Russell hustled her out of the bathroom to where her shoes were set next to her couch. As she slipped the Jimmy Choos on, he pulled her coat out of the front closet.

Just as she had finished buttoning it up, someone knocked on the door. They looked at each other.

"Would that be the car service?" she asked as she strolled to the door.

"No. They'd call me and wait downstairs." Russell frowned.

Pushing up on her toes, she peered through the peephole then smiled. "It's Lucercio."

"Oh good." Russell sounded like he was grinding his teeth, but Bridget ignored his sarcastic tone.

Bridget yanked open the door then threw her arms around the tall blond man before he could say anything. Lucercio embraced her, crushing her against his chest while burying his face in her hair. Once she stepped away, he smiled down at her.

"Are you coming to the opening with us?" she asked as she stepped back.

"No. I have business to deal with and I actually didn't know your show opened tonight." He inclined his head toward Russell, but didn't say anything to him.

It surprised her that there seemed to be such animosity between the two men in her life. Of course, Russell thought Lucercio wanted her money, which was ridiculous considering how rich she assumed he was. So Lucercio resented Russell's assumptions.

Aside from that, though, she had no idea what else Lucercio thought about Russell. He'd never made any kind of comment and his attitude toward Russell was the same as any other person—utter distain.

"I just thought I'd stop by to see how you were doing. The last time we talked, you didn't sound okay." He gestured toward the various canvases scattered around the studio portion of her flat. "And I see that my feelings were right."

She glanced over to them then pursed her lips. "How do you know I wasn't painting kittens and rainbows?"

Snorting, Lucercio cupped her face in his hands. "Because, Bridget my dear, kittens and rainbows don't exist in your creative realm. Those are for moments when you're in the real world, surrounded by mortals and the terrible things they do to each other. You need things to make you smile."

He always made comments like that, and she never really understood what he meant by them. It was almost as if he held nothing but contempt for people, yet he never treated her with anything but respect.

"You're right. It's more of the same." She strolled over to one of the canvases before turning it around for him to see.

His sharp inhalation told her that she'd surprised him. Looking at the half-finished painting, she didn't see what might have upset him. All she could make out was a man kneeling on a rocky precipice. His long hair hung around his head, hiding his face as he bowed in front of another person. Bridget hadn't blocked or sketched the other one out—he hadn't come to her yet. Only his general height and that he was male. The impression in her mind, though, was that he'd be holding a sword to the kneeling man's back.

Red stripes covered the cowed man's back, as though someone had cut strips from his flesh. His battered hands rested on his thighs, clenched so tight that his knuckles were white. Despair rode the man, causing his shoulders to droop.

Bridget had been crying when she'd surfaced after painting the scene, her heart heavy with sadness for the wounded man.

"That's moving," Lucercio spoke softly as he lifted his hand, almost touching the canvas but stopping an inch from it. "When you are finished, I would like to purchase it."

"You know you don't have to pay for it. You can have it when I'm done." Bridget tilted her head to study him. "It touches you. Why?"

"I've known despair like he has. In some ways, I've been where that man has been, on my knees, bleeding but defiant to the end." Lucercio's voice was low and gentle as he explained.

She wanted to know more. Lucercio didn't speak about his past. He'd shown up one night during one of her deeper breaks with reality. He'd gotten her home, cleaned her up, and stayed with her until she'd come back to herself.

Aside from Russell, Lucercio was her other family. She didn't remember her parents, who'd died when she was very young. There were no other members and Bridget didn't make friends easily either. Heck, it was difficult to do so when she didn't know if she was going to lose her mind at any minute.

"Bridget, I'm sorry, but we must leave if we're going to get to the gallery in time," Russell spoke up, and for the first time, she did hear a tone of apology in his voice.

Lucercio bowed his head slightly before meeting her gaze. "You go and have a good time. Try not to panic, and remember to be nice to people. Not all of them want to look at the crazy artist. Most of them see your talent and are in awe of you."

She gave him a skeptical grin, but let him lead her from her apartment while Russell followed them. Waiting by the lift, she watched Russell lock her door before joining them. Lucercio tucked her hand in the crook of his elbow as they stepped into the car to ride down to the first floor.

Silence filled the lift and she leaned against Lucercio, absorbing his warmth and strength for the upcoming ordeal. She wasn't a people person, and having to mingle and schmooze them to get them to buy her artwork was demanding for her. But Russell knew that and he would do his best to get her through the night.

"How did I get so lucky?"

Both men looked at her with questions in their eyes.

"To end up with two wonderful men as friends," she informed them.

Russell shared a glance with Lucercio before shrugging. "Just a reward for being such a good person."

She waited to hear Lucercio snort or say something sarcastic, but her friend didn't say anything disparaging. "Do you believe that?"

He brushed a kiss over her cheek. "Of course, I do, honey. You're one of the only people in this god-forsaken world I want to spend time with."

"Thank you both for dealing with my craziness and weirdness." She hugged Lucercio's arm to her chest then flashed a bright smile at Russell. "You've got me through a lot of years when I never thought I'd be able to take any more."

"Us and your painting," Russell pointed out, seeming to not want to take all the credit. "I just wish I knew why you had those fugue states and what all those scenes you see while in them mean."

The lift slowed to a stop then the doors opened. She walked through the lobby to the front where the doorman opened it.

"You're looking radiant tonight, Miss Langston," he said as she passed him.

"Thank you, Jones." She flashed him a smile.

"Here's the car." Russell motioned toward a black limo idling at the curb. The driver climbed out before walking around to open the car door.

Bridget embraced Lucercio. "If you have some free time tomorrow, come see me. I'd like to chat and maybe I'll have more of the painting done by then."

He tucked her under his chin for a second, holding her tight. Then he stepped away. "I'll do that. Have fun tonight."

Another slight bow to Russell then Lucercio stalked down the pavement. Bridget watched him and noticed how people flowed to one side or the other of him. No one seemed to want to touch or even meet eyes with him as he walked away.

"He's a very intimidating man," Russell muttered as he ushered Bridget into the car.

"I know, but he's also one of the nicest men I know." She settled onto the seat after making sure that her dress wouldn't wrinkle when she sat.

Russell didn't make a sound, but she could see he didn't believe her. "I'm sure he's nice to you, but the rest of the world is scared silly of him."

"Do you know anything about him? I know you checked him out." Bridget didn't look at her friend. She kept her gaze out of the window as the lights of London rushed by her.

"He checks out just fine. He seems to be exactly what he wants us to think he is, but I'm pretty sure there's a hell of a lot more going on with him than we'll ever know."

She didn't argue about that. Ever since they'd met ten years ago, he'd been a constant in her life. Oh he wasn't always by her side, but somehow he was always there in her mind and heart. Like the other day, he'd talked to her, getting her back to her flat without any more incidents. Bridget had never asked about how she could hear him in her head because it was just another one of those things—like her visions and her fugues.

"Lucercio is very private," she said.

Russell squeezed her hand but didn't comment. As they continued through the streets of London, Bridget took deep breaths to steady her nerves. She wished that she could have a drink or two, but alcohol tended to make things worse for her. She'd learned that the hard way.

"We're here," Russell informed her as the driver slowed to pull up to the curb in front of Russell's gallery.

Taking another deep breath, she squared her shoulders then stepped from the limo after the driver opened the door for her. Bridget waited for Russell to join her on the pavement before she walked into the gallery. They still had an hour before the show opened, which would give her time to adjust to being outside her safety zone.

"Thank God you're here." Jordan, one of Russell's personal assistants, came rushing up. "We need you to decide where this last picture should be hung."

"I thought I gave you the layout for the show." Russell glanced over at Bridget.

Smiling, she waved him away. "Go. Take care of the emergency. I'm going to wander around to look at the canvases and see how you placed them."

He gave her an air kiss then bustled off with Jordan in tow. There were glasses and a pitcher of water on a small table just inside the gallery, so Bridget poured herself some before heading out to stroll through the gallery.

Russell had exclusive rights to sell her paintings. She rarely had shows in other cities, or countries for that matter, because any change in her schedule could throw her off. So when she did have a showing at Walvoski Gallery, it tended to be a big deal.

Bridget didn't know why her paintings were so popular and why people were willing to pay so much for them. When the experience had started, she'd figured that her art would be a fifteen-minute wonder, yet the demand was almost more than she could fulfill.

There were other artists in the show as well. She'd told Russell that she wanted him to pick an up-and-coming artist to be shown with her — Bridget wanted someone else to get a chance to reach the eyes of the patrons or buyers. She was more than willing to share the limelight.

A talented young artist had done the small watercolors Bridget noticed in the first two rooms she'd walked through. She stood in front of one that portrayed Tower Bridge all lit up at midnight. It touched a place inside her, since she'd spent many nights on the banks of the Thames staring at that sight.

After a quick check to make sure that it hadn't been sold, she went in search of Russell. She found her friend supervising the hanging of one of her largest paintings. She wasn't about to bother him at that moment, so she waited. When he'd finished, he turned to see her standing there.

"Can I help you, Bridget?"

"Yes, I want to purchase a painting." She gestured back toward the room she'd come from.

"Really? I'm impressed that someone caught your eye. You're very hard to please." Russell walked up to her then offered her his arm.

"It's a sight I've seen so many times it's burnt into my brain. But whoever painted it gave it a kind of light I haven't seen before." She pointed toward the Tower Bridge painting. "I made sure it wasn't sold."

"I'll mark it, so no one else can get it. Now go and see how your canvases look. If you see any in spots you don't like, let me know and I'll change them." Russell tapped her hand and smiled.

"It's too close to the opening for you to be rearranging my stuff." Bridget shrugged. "It'll be beautiful like always."

"Are you hungry? You should go grab some refreshments before people start arriving, dear girl. We don't want you to pass out during the opening." He winked at her and she giggled.

"That was terrible, wasn't it?"

She'd done that once and the tabloids had blown it all out of proportion, saying that she'd been high and had passed out from an overdose. It had been low blood sugar, but that wasn't sensational enough to sell copies.

"Mr Walvoski, I just have one more question." Jordan came back.

"Certainly. Do you happen to have a sold sticker?"

Jordan pulled a sheet out of his pocket before handing it over to Russell. Bridget watched as he put a sticker on the card next to the Tower Bridge watercolor.

"Thank you, Russell."

"You're welcome, dear."

Leaving Russell to organize Jordan, Bridget wandered off, heading to the hors d'oeuvres set up on tables at the back of the gallery. It was a brilliant idea, forcing the attending art lovers to peruse the items for sale while they made their way to the foods.

After setting her empty glass down, she filled a small plate then took herself over to a café table in the corner, not wanting to get in the way of the employees doing last minute touches. One of the waiters brought her a glass of water and she gave him a slight nod. Just as she had finished eating, Russell came back to get her.

"Are you ready? It's time to unlock the doors and let your adoring public in."

"Adoring public? Let's not stretch the truth, Russell. Like I said, most of them are here to see what crazy thing I'll do next."

After standing, she brushed the wrinkles out of her dress and fluffed her curls. "Do I look okay?"

"You look beautiful as always. Just like an angel."

"A fallen one, perhaps," she joked.

A strange gleam of red light shined in Russell's eyes for a second, but when Bridget blinked, it went away. "Trust me, honey. You aren't a fallen angel."

The utter surety and seriousness in Russell's voice caught Bridget a little off guard. She'd just been teasing, yet it seemed as though Russell had believed her.

"Do you believe in angels?" She had to ask.

"I believe in a lot of things that most people don't," Russell replied, but before she could ask anything else, he said, "Come now. We have to go to the front and greet the customers."

Bridget let him take her hand, though she made a note to come back to the conversation when they weren't so busy.

Chapter Five

Mika'il appeared in the alleyway just across from the Walvoski Gallery. He straightened his tie before tugging on the cuffs of his shirt to make sure that the proper length was showing from his jacket sleeves. The diamond cufflinks gleamed in the street lights, as did the tie pin he wore.

He watched as a trio of people walked into the brightly lit building and he tried to decide why he'd agreed to meet the others here. Hanging with Enforcers and mortals wasn't his usual way of spending his spare time. Not that he got any downtime. There was almost always something going on in the world that needed the archangel's attention.

Mika'il didn't resent it because, for most of his existence, it was all he'd known. Maybe God regretted having given Mika'il a chance at being mortal for a while and letting him catch a glimpse of the way humans loved each other.

Yet could God ever really regret anything he did? There had to be a good reason why he'd allowed his highest-ranking angel to become mortal. Mika'il had never worked up the courage to ask him because really, the only creature besides man who had ever asked God why he did something was Lucifer, and Mika'il had seen how well that had turned out.

"Are you going in?"

He whirled to see Lucifer behind him, shoulder propped against the brick wall. His hands were stuffed in the pockets of his black wool overcoat. There was a casual air about him that worried Mika'il. The fallen rarely seemed relaxed, so to see him like that put Mika'il on edge.

"What are you doing here?"

Lucifer shook his head. "I asked first."

Huffing in annoyance, Mika'il glanced back at the gallery. "I'm trying to decide what I was thinking when I told them I'd come."

"You were thinking you were lonely and it was a good way to spend the evening. The world isn't particularly crazy tonight," Lucifer pointed out.

Mika'il didn't like how close to the truth Lucifer had gotten. Turning to face Lucifer fully, he folded his arms over his chest and stared at the fallen. "What are you doing here?"

Shrugging, Lucifer glanced up and down the alley. "I'm just hanging out in an alley. Isn't that where most people meet the Devil?"

"Maybe, but you wouldn't be caught dead in a place like this usually, so what are you doing in this one?" Mika'il asked once more.

"Just watching how the other half lives." Lucifer inclined his head in the direction of the gallery. "I'm amazed by what mortals consider art and how it touches their souls. Each sees something different in the splashes of paint or swirl of color."

"What do you see when you look at paintings?"

Lucifer's expression went blank. "I see nothing. You need a soul to be touched by art of any kind, and we both know I don't have a soul anymore." He pushed himself off the wall to stand straight. He took his hands out of his pocket then clasped them behind his back. "Your friends are waiting for you."

"Why did you help Nevan and Cassandra? Why were you *even* friends with Cassandra?"

He looked shocked, but Mika'il could tell it was an act by the gleam in Lucifer's dark eyes. "Who said I was friends with her? I simply stopped by to talk to her from time to time. She was one of the few who hadn't turned away from me after the Fall. That doesn't make us friends."

"But you saved her and Nevan back in Los Angeles. You came to take the soul of the man torturing him." Mika'il didn't know why he was pressing the issue. If Lucifer didn't want to tell him the truth, he wouldn't, and it wasn't as though he could believe the fallen anyway.

"Ah... There's the truth. I came to take his soul because he went back on our deal. Not because I had any feelings for Cassandra or that rather unusual mortal she fell in love with." Anger flashed in Lucifer's eyes. "No one welches on me."

Mika'il snorted, but didn't reply to that. He had to admit that the thought of Lucifer helping them out of the goodness of his heart was such a stretch that Mika'il had to be crazy to believe it.

Lucifer released a low puff of air before motioning to the street. "Your friends are here. You should go and have some fun. Plus, you never know what you might see while you're in there. Maybe some art will strike your fancy."

"And where would I hang said art? It's not like I keep a flat here in the city, or in any city in the world."

"You never know. Maybe you would take it back to your office in Purgatory and hang it there." Lucifer smiled and Mika'il's heart broke a little at the pain in it. "I must go attend to my business. You go have fun and keep your heart receptive."

After saying that, Lucifer vanished, causing Mika'il to grimace at the cryptic message. Why was it that every time the fallen left lately, he'd say things like that? If Mika'il didn't know better, he'd swear that Lucifer knew something he didn't, and that just wasn't possible.

Making his way across the street and up to the gallery door, he kept a lookout for Joan or any of the others. He'd thought he'd seen them go in while he had been talking to Lucifer, but now he couldn't see any of them in the midst of the large crowd.

A young woman holding a clipboard stopped him. "Sir, I need to see your invitation."

He glanced at her, knowing he could use his power to make her think she'd seen it, but he didn't like to waste it on trivial things like that. "I'm meeting some friends and one of them has my invitation."

"Certainly, sir. Who are you meeting?" She didn't look convinced.

Were unwanted people trying to sneak into gallery openings that big an issue? Mika'il was about to ask, when he heard Dominic call to him.

"Mika'il, we weren't sure you were going to show up. Fashionably late, I see." Dominic smiled at the woman as he handed her an off-white card. "Here is Mika'il's invitation."

"Thank you, Mr LaFontaine. And thank you for joining us, Mr Angel." Her arched eyebrows went up as she said his last name.

He inclined his head slightly before following Dominic farther into the gallery itself.

"Angel? William came up with that one, didn't he?" Mika'il took a glass of champagne off one of the trays passing by.

"What makes you say that? We'd forgotten to ask you for a name earlier today, so we improvised." Dominic chuckled. "It fits, though it's not likely anyone will be asking you your name. Come on. The others are in the bigger rooms closer to the back of the gallery. Those are the canvases we all came to see."

"I'll be there in a minute." A watercolor caught his eye. "I want to check these out."

Dominic looked around and nodded. "All right. These are nice, but I'm not a fan of watercolors."

Mika'il waved him away before he edged closer to the art. So many scenes of modern London were hanging on the walls. He'd never seen watercolors look so realistic. Tower Bridge and the Tower of London were painted like he would see them on a foggy day. A little faded around the edges, yet the lines of building and bridge were crisp and clean.

He did wish he had a place to hang them, but the Waiting Room wasn't meant to make people feel comfortable about what had happened to them and where they were going. It was simply a stopgap between Heaven and Hell. He'd never felt the urge to decorate it.

Wandering slowly from canvas to canvas, he couldn't help overhearing the bits and pieces of conversations going on around him.

"They say she's crazy."

"She wanders off for days and when they find her, she's dirty and muttering."

"Why are the most creative people the craziest? Do you think her paintings are examples of the demons who haunt her memories?"

Frowning, he tried to block out what they were saying, but the gossiping and chatter continued. Mika'il wondered if the artist could hear them. What was it about mental illness that made other people think they could talk about the person? It was almost as if once they found out a person was—or might be—mentally ill, that person also became blind and deaf. No one thought there was anything wrong about discussing them like they were animals put on display in a cage at a zoo.

He wanted to say something, but realized he might be a little more sensitive to the situation because of his own history. Having once been deemed insane and separated from the world he knew had had a profound effect on him, even if it wasn't a world he lived in usually.

After emptying his glass, he set it on a tray before taking another. It didn't matter how much he had to drink, he didn't get drunk, but he fitted in better if he held something in his hand.

"Mika'il, you need to get back here." Celeste's voice echoed through his head and he could hear her distress.

"On my way."

Mika'il pushed his way through the crowd, doing his best not to knock people out of the way or bring more attention to himself than normal. He could've cloaked his passage through the humans, but it wasn't worth it.

He found the others standing at the back wall of the gallery, staring up at the biggest canvas in the show. The painting was seven feet tall and when he saw what was on it, he almost dropped his glass.

"Holy shit." William's curse was soft yet all of them heard it.

"How did she know?" Danielle's voice wobbled with sadness and pain.

"Is the artist one of us?" Christian glanced around, seemingly searching for the person who'd painted it.

Mika'il couldn't speak. His throat had closed from an overload of horror, agony and rage. The life-sized painting depicted a winged warrior holding his sword aloft and standing in front of a set of golden gates. His silver eyes were cold and empty on the surface, but when Mika'il looked closer, he saw hurt and disappointment lurking. It was apparent that he was blocking the gates, not allowing someone to enter them.

Hell, the way the angel's eyes seemed to move, it was as if he looked at each person in the room, found them wanting, and denied them access to their deepest desires. Tears welled in Mika'il's eyes and he blinked, not wanting to cry in front of hundreds of people.

Celeste buried her face in Adam's shoulder and Danielle did the same to Grant. The men stood there, frozen, as one of the worst days of their long lives rose up in front of them like a condemnation.

"Was this what it was like when you were banished?" Joan asked softly, obviously not wanting any of the other humans to hear them talking.

William nodded. "You can't see the horde of fallen angels standing there, begging Mika'il to let us in."

"That's you?" Abby pointed at the winged angel before looking over at Mika'il.

He nodded, but didn't say anything. He wasn't sure that he could speak at that moment. As horrifying as that day had been for the fallen, it had been just as devastating for him.

"Is it weird that I've never pictured any of you with wings?" Grant mentioned. He waited for a moment and when no one answered him, he said, "You're right. It is weird, especially after finding Ferguson's skeleton. He still had his wings."

"Who is the artist? How can they know down to the tiniest detail what that day was like?" Dominic shot Mika'il a glance. "Maybe we should check out the rest of the paintings."

Mika'il wasn't sure he wanted to do that. What else was hanging on these walls to surprise them? He needed to find the artist. When he spread his power out over the attendees, he sensed several other fallen and a few other Enforcers, but none that he didn't know. And the person who'd created these images wasn't among them.

"Mika'il, come here," Teresa called out.

Closing his eyes, he took a deep breath, shoring up his courage to see what she wanted to show him. When he opened them, he turned to see where she stood then went to her. He looked at the painting and his jaw dropped.

It was him again. Only this time he stood in the clearing of the hedge maze at the County Asylum of Northumberland. His head was thrown back as he stared up at the blue sky. The angel fountain was in the background, though this one wasn't done in marble. It looked as though a living person was standing there, tears streaming from her face into the basin she held.

"Bridget," he murmured, reaching out to touch the angel's face but stopping inches from the canvas.

"Is that the woman you fell in love with?" Joan took his hand in hers before anyone said something about him trying to touch the artwork.

Mika'il didn't notice her holding his hand or anything except the bright blue eyes of the woman in the painting. "Yes. That's Bridget exactly as I remember her."

"And how you looked back then," she enquired.

He nodded. "That's the spot where we first met and where we spent as much of our time together as we could when we were allowed outside."

"Joan, bring him over here," Christian said and Mika'il didn't protest as she led him away from that painting to a café table in the corner of the gallery.

Christian pushed him down into a chair then handed him a drink. "I know this won't do much, but drink. It might help a little with the shock. I have to admit if I was a drinker, even as an Enforcer, I'd be buying a bottle by now."

"You're in almost every one of these paintings," Dominic informed him as the others joined them.

"I don't understand how that's possible. It's as if the artist knows me personally and has seen me both as archangel and as human. I checked and aside from the usual fallen and Enforcers that I'm familiar with, there isn't any stranger here." Mika'il gestured to the gaggle of humans milling around the room. "They are human, nothing special about them at all."

"Yet one of them knows you well enough to depict you in your natural form."

Something in William's tone made Mika'il shoot to his feet. "Is there a painting of me naked?"

"How well did you get to know Bridget back in the asylum?" William's blue eyes twinkled with enjoyment when Mika'il blushed.

"We were consenting adults, William, and I wasn't an archangel then." Mika'il scrubbed one of his trembling hands over his face. "She knew exactly what was going on. I never took advantage of her."

"He's not saying you did. He's simply obnoxious." Abby elbowed her husband and glared at him.

"I'd heard such wonderful things about this artist. She's becoming quite popular because of her paintings of angels. I just never thought she'd be painting pictures of Mika'il or any of the rest of you." Joan shook her head. "Though there is one of Christian that I'm going to buy."

"The artist is a woman?"

Could it be? But how had she survived all those centuries with the visions and dreams haunting her every waking minute? The world is cruel to those who are different or perceived as weak.

Joan nodded as she snagged a catalog off one of the other tables. She flipped through the pages until she came to the bio. "Here. While you're reading that, I'm going to flag down one of the gallery workers to get a sold sticker on the one of Christian."

"Wait a minute. Show me. I haven't seen that one." Christian followed his wife toward one of the other rooms.

"Are we in any of the other ones?" Dominic asked the rest while Mika'il read the bio.

"B Langston has been painting pictures of angels since she was a child. She says they come to her in dreams and are as vivid then as they turn out on the

canvas. 'I truly believe angels watch over all of us.'"
He wanted to see what she looked like, but there
wasn't a picture anywhere in the catalog. "Why isn't
there a picture of her in this?"

Dominic shrugged. "Maybe she prefers a little
privacy, but she should be here. The artists are usually
present at show openings so patrons can meet them.
Makes the people who are paying thousands of
dollars for art feel special to act like they are personal
friends with the artist."

Mika'il rolled his eyes. "That's silly."

"Hey, if you were spending as much money as some
of these people are on these paintings, you might want
to feel important for a minute or two as well. Besides,
it helps stroke the artist's ego to hear how much
someone loves their work." Danielle rested her hands
on her hips as she turned in a circle. "I thought I saw
the owner of the gallery around here a few minutes
ago. I got an introduction to him earlier in the night
because I did a consultation on a Rembrandt for one of
his colleagues."

"Yes, let's find the owner. He'll know who the artist
is and be able to introduce us." Mika'il jumped to his
feet, his need to meet the artist almost overwhelming.

"Whoa. You need to rein yourself in, Mika'il. You're
going to scare the poor man if you go at him like that."
Grant touched his arm. "You have to remember he's a
mere mortal and to suddenly have the man in the
paintings appear like magic in front of him might
freak him out. Why don't you let Danielle talk to
him?"

"Because I have to ask him myself." He didn't know
if he could explain why it was so important that he
hear the information with his own ears, straight from
the owner's mouth. It just was.

"How can you not sense this B Langston? I would've thought you'd be able to pick her out in the middle of a thousand people." William frowned.

Mika'il shrugged. "I don't know. It's like whenever I think of her, there's a blank wall between us. Almost like she didn't exist or something, which is odd because obviously she exists, she painted those pictures right?"

All of his friends stared at him, and he realized it was the first time they'd ever seen him completely lose his cool. The only other person who'd ever seen that was Lucifer, and usually that was because he had caused it. Turning to face away from them, Mika'il closed his eyes, took a deep breath, and gathered his power to him. It helped to calm him down.

When he was ready, he met Danielle's gaze. "Let's go find this guy."

She nodded before turning around to weave her way through the crowd. Mika'il stayed close behind her, trying not to shove people out of the way. She approached a shorter, dark-haired man wearing a black velvet jacket and a bright red silk vest.

As he spotted them approaching him, he smiled at Danielle, but his happiness disappeared when he looked over her shoulder and saw Mika'il standing there. The man's dark eyes flashed red, causing Mika'il to stop where he was.

"A true demon." He hissed.

Chapter Six

The demon dropped his gaze then bowed his head. "Sir."

"You own this gallery?" Before the demon could answer, Mika'il said, "You can look at me. I hate when people act like I'm so scary they can't bear to face me. I have nothing against you."

"You are scary, sir. You, more than anyone aside from Lucifer himself, are terrifying to creatures like us," the demon spoke quietly then glanced around.

"Is there somewhere we can talk privately?" He didn't want to frighten the creature but he had questions he needed answers to. "I'm Mika'il."

"I know."

"You might know who I am, but I don't know the name you go by now."

The demon frowned before he said, "I'm Russell Walvoski."

Mika'il didn't offer his hand, knowing that Russell wouldn't take it. He turned to look at Danielle. "Did you know he was a true demon?"

She shook her head. "I don't have the talent to sense them. Sorry. If I had known, I wouldn't have brought you to him. No need to upset either of you."

"If you'll follow me, sir." Russell gestured toward a set of stairs. "We can go talk in my office."

"I'll go find the others and see what other paintings of ourselves we can discover." Danielle left them before either of them could tell her not to go.

"I guess we're on our own," Mika'il muttered.

"Oh goodie," Russell murmured then shot Mika'il an anxious glance.

He chuckled. "I know I'm not someone you want to spend time with, Russell, but I really do have some questions for you. I promise I have no interest in hurting you. As far as I know, you haven't done anything that needs punishment."

Russell escorted him upstairs to his office then shut the door behind them so that they wouldn't be interrupted. Mika'il took the chair the demon gestured toward. Once Russell was settled behind his desk, the tension between them eased slightly.

"What can I do for you, sir?" Russell folded his hands together. His tone said that he was eager to help out, but his expression said that he just wanted it over with.

"I need to know who painted those pictures." Mika'il fought against the urge to grab Russell and shake him until he spilled everything.

Russell's gaze landed on everything in the office except Mika'il. "Why?"

He shot him a surprised look. "Why? I have every right to know who's painting pictures of my friends and me."

"What pictures?"

"Now that's just being obtuse." Mika'il shook his head. "I don't want to make you tell me, but I will if I have to. Russell, there are several canvases with my likeness on them. I know for sure there's at least one with Christian, since his wife is buying it."

Russell swallowed and Mika'il could tell that the demon was seriously considering not telling him. Mika'il sat straight in the chair, letting a little of his power leak out. Russell hissed and shrank back.

"Fine, but if you hurt her, I'll do everything in my power to destroy you."

"Are you seriously threatening me?" He couldn't believe what he was hearing coming from the true demon.

"Yes. You might kill me, but I don't care. I will protect her with my life. It's bad enough that creature comes around all the time. Now I'm going to have to deal with you as well. I haven't ever done anything wrong in the thousands of years I've been on this Earth. Why am I being tortured by angels?"

Russell snarled, but Mika'il wasn't afraid of him. Why would he be, since he was the strongest angel in heaven? He'd faced down Lucifer Daystar and had stood firm when the fallen had come to the gate to beg for forgiveness.

The only thing he'd ever been afraid of was disappointing God. No true demon would ever make him cower. He surged to his feet then took one step forward to brace his hands on the desk. He leaned over to put his face right in Russell's.

"Don't you dare threaten me, demon. I've dealt with your kind from the moment of your creation. You don't scare me. I can destroy you with a thought," he growled.

To his surprise, Russell didn't back down. In fact, he pushed to his feet and stood inches away from Mika'il. "I know you can, but I don't care. I love that girl and she's gone through hell all of her life. She doesn't need you bothering her about why she's painting you. Why can't you just let it go?"

"I can't let it go because she's painting scenes of a part of my life where I lost the only thing that ever mattered more to me than God when I was mortal. How does she know these things? Who is she and how does she know me? Is she here tonight? I want to meet her."

Russell blinked before slowly sinking back into his chair. "Oh my God."

Mika'il felt his eye twitch at Russell's use of God like that, but he let it go because he saw the shock in the demon's face. "What's so shocking about that? That I could fall in love with someone? That I could find joy in a mortal?"

"You're him."

"I'm who?" Now Russell wasn't making sense.

"I really thought that he was the guy, but while he does come around a lot, he never seemed to look at her like you'd think a guy would look at the woman he loved, you know?"

"I don't know what you're talking about. You knew about me."

Russell shook his head. "No. I knew about the man in the paintings. She sees him in her visions and dreams all the time. She doesn't know why she sees him. Hell, she doesn't understand why she has to paint all these scenes and things." He pressed his hand to his mouth. "I'm not sure she'll be able to handle meeting you. How do I tell her that she's been dreaming of the most powerful archangel in heaven? I mean, she tells me that she believes in Heaven and Hell. That angels and demons haunt the world she finds herself in at times. She even considers *him* an angel, even though I know he's not even close to being one."

"Who are you talking about?" Mika'il's mind spun. Listening to Russell babble was going to drive him insane and he had never thought that would happen while he was an angel. Especially after having to deal with Lucifer all the time.

"Umm... No one important." Russell winced after he had said it as though whoever he had been talking about could hear him. "Just a friend of hers."

"Are you going to tell me who she is or am I going to have to read your mind?" Mika'il didn't really want to do that. He often went into the minds of his Enforcers to talk to them, but he tried not to rummage through them because he didn't want to know what they were thinking or feeling every minute of every day.

Russell took a deep breath then said, "Let me talk to her first. If you just show up on her doorstep, you're going to freak her out and she's just come home after being on the streets for several days. I don't want to cause her distress by having you appear out of the blue."

"I wouldn't do anything to hurt her. I just want to know who she is," he protested.

"You will, but I want to prepare her first. Come back here tomorrow morning and I'll tell you. Well, I'll tell you only if she wants you to know. If she doesn't, then I guess you're going to have to read my mind because I won't go against her wishes on this." Russell squared his chin and the look on his face told Mika'il that

Russell had given as much as he was going to on the subject at the moment.

Mika'il straightened then tugged on his sleeves to get his jacket to hang just right. "I guess if that's all you're going to offer me at the moment, I'll have to take it. Your artist isn't here, is she?"

"Not anymore. She was getting upset because some people were harassing her about her situation. I told her to go home and paint. Putting oil on canvas always makes her feel better about things. I just hope she'll be there when I stop by tonight because if she's not, I don't know if I'll be able to find her and it's supposed to rain later." Russell looked worried.

"Your client seems rather fragile," he commented as he strolled to the door.

Russell's smile glowed and Mika'il could see the love the demon had for the mystery woman. "She's the strongest mortal I know. To go through everything she's gone through and to be as sane as she is amazes me. I just don't want to inflict more pain if I don't have to."

"I'll be back here first thing tomorrow morning to find out who she is. I give you my word that I won't go looking for her tonight." Mika'il sighed. "I still have to go through the gallery and see all of the paintings. Find out what else she's seen while having visions."

"Some of her stuff is quite disturbing," Russell admitted.

Mika'il sighed as he opened the door. "If she's seen half of what I've seen in my life, there should be nightmares hanging on the walls downstairs."

After leaving the office, he went down to wander through the gallery again. This time he stopped and looked at each painting and his interest in the artist grew the longer he spent there.

* * * *

Russell wiped his hand over his mouth after Mika'il had walked out. He let his head drop to his desk and groaned. Why did this have to happen now? What the hell was the archangel doing in London and what had driven him to come to the gallery on this particular night?

It wasn't until he'd seen Mika'il standing behind Danielle Carson that he'd realized the man who starred so prominently in most of Bridget's paintings was actually the warrior archangel and the most power being in the world aside from God himself.

Maybe he should've gotten a clue when all her scenes featured angels and angelic imagery, but there were also those garden scenes as well. Those had thrown him off because they were so normal and lovely. Even though they were obviously set in a different era, Russell had wished that Bridget had known a love like that shown in them.

"I can't let it go because she's painting scenes of a part of my life where I lost the only thing that ever mattered more to me than God."

What had Mika'il meant when he'd said that? Had those normal scenes been real? Could Bridget be hooking into the memories of the archangel? If so, why did she always include herself in those paintings? There was one where Mika'il and she were dancing under a full moon. Russell had commented on how in love the two of them looked and Bridget had smiled then told him that it had been the best night of her life.

When he'd questioned her about it later, she had said she must have misspoken and it was obviously the best night of that woman's life. Bridget didn't have any idea of why she'd remember these things in exact detail, though she told him she often had moments where she would smell a certain cologne. She'd look around for the man who wore it because she remembered how much that man meant to her.

After pushing to his feet, Russell walked around to leave his office. He locked the door then went downstairs to find Jordan. When he found his assistant, he pulled him aside.

"I'm leaving you in charge. Something important has come up. You know how to take care of things here and I'll deal with the sales when I come in tomorrow."

"Yes, sir. Is everything okay?" Jordan looked concerned.

"Everything's fine. Just some business I forgot to take care of earlier and unfortunately, it can't be left undone tonight." Russell patted Jordan's shoulder. "I trust you to do your job, Jordan. I'll see you in the morning."

Jordan nodded, and Russell did know he could trust the mortal to do what Russell had trained him to do. Once that was taken care of, he went outside to wave down a cab. After he'd settled in the back seat and had given the driver Bridget's address, he pulled out his phone to call her. He didn't want to drop in on her unannounced tonight. She'd been a little freaked out by something when he'd sent her home.

Had she seen Mika'il and, not knowing who he was, panicked about the fact that she'd been dreaming about him all of her life? Or had something else happened while he had been busy with other patrons?

"Hello." She didn't sound upset when she answered.

"Hello, Bridget. I was calling to let you know I'm on my way over to your flat," he announced.

"Okay. Why? I'm doing fine. I don't think I'll be having an episode tonight." She sounded tired. "I was hoping to go to bed early. I didn't get much sleep last night."

He chuckled. "I know, dear, and I promise I won't stay long. I need to talk to you about something that came up after you left. It's no big deal or anything."

It was a very big deal, but he didn't want to say anything right then. He knew she'd think and worry about it until she worked herself up. Then she wouldn't be any good to him when he got there.

"All right, since you're on your way already. Just use your key and I'll put the tea on." She hung up.

He tucked the phone back and smiled as he looked out of the window. Putting the tea on. Somehow she knew that whatever he wanted to talk to her about would take longer than he had said. There would be tea, biscuits, and possibly scones, if she had any left.

There had been a lot of tea and biscuits consumed between them in the years since he'd discovered her. In the early years, he would go over to her little flat whenever she called him—day or night. As a true demon, he didn't need to sleep, so staying up with her wasn't difficult for him.

The driver pulled up in front of Bridget's building, so Russell climbed out after paying the man. He made his way up to her flat before letting himself in.

"Bridget, it's just me," he called as he hung his jacket up in the closet. He removed his vest as well then unbuttoned his collar while wandering over to her kitchen area.

"I'll be right out," she yelled from the bathroom.

He hummed as he checked on the tea steeping in her china teapot. It was almost ready, so he'd give it another minute or two before he poured it. Checking the boxes on the counter, he found the scones and biscuits.

"Making yourself at home, I see," Bridget said as she walked over to him. She kissed his cheeks then picked up the tray with the pot and cups on it. "Let's go sit on the couch and you can tell me what has you so worried."

"I'm not worried," he protested weakly.

She shot him an amused look. "Russell, I've known you a long time. I know what you look and sound like when you're worried. I heard it in your voice when you called. You didn't want to say anything before you got here because you didn't want me to freak out. As you can see, I'm fine."

Russell rolled his eyes yet he didn't argue with her as he followed her with the food. He waited until she had chosen which end to sit on then he took the other. While they doctored their tea the way they wanted it, he tried to figure out the best way to tell her about Mika'il. He couldn't tell her that he was the archangel. She wouldn't believe that, no matter how much she believed in angels. Once everything was just the way they both liked it, Bridget leaned back against the arm of the couch and looked at him.

"All right, Russell. We have our tea and cookies. Now tell me what wasn't so important that you came all the way to my place to talk to me about it." She studied him over the rim of her cup.

He cleared his throat. "I had a request from a patron to meet you."

"After I left?"

"Yes. I told him you weren't feeling well, which is why you left the showing so early. He wanted to know if he could meet you some time." He fidgeted with the scone on his plate. "I told him I'd talk to you and it would be your decision."

"What can you tell me about him? Do you know him?" She sipped her tea casually but Russell could see the faint tremor in her hand.

"He is a very nice man. I trust him not to hurt you in any way. He simply wishes to discuss some of the paintings with you."

Chapter Seven

Bridget wished that her hands didn't shake, but she couldn't stop. There seemed to be something fateful about this man wanting to meet her right now. She'd been unsure about letting Russell show these particular canvases because they were the closest to her heart, but she didn't have the room to keep them all, and what was the point of hoarding them? All the scenes they portrayed, she could vividly recreate any time she wanted to.

"Which paintings does he want to talk about?"

Russell shifted where he sat, and she could tell that he wasn't happy about coming to her with the request.

"If you didn't want to tell me about him, why did you?"

"Because he's the type of guy who, if I didn't come and ask you to see him, would find you himself. I didn't want him showing up on your doorstep without you getting fair warning."

"Fair warning? Is he dangerous?"

Russell nodded. "Oh yes. He's dangerous to our peace of mind, and other things."

A shiver of fear ran down her spine. "If he's that dangerous, shouldn't we talk to the police or something?"

"No, dear. He could be that dangerous, but I know he couldn't do anything to you, even if he were angry. It's me that I'm worried about." Russell grimaced. "Though I must admit, I trust him much more than I would ever trust Lucercio."

"Hey, now. Lucercio has never done anything to you." That she knew of. "This other guy seems much worse. I'm not sure I want to see him now, after listening to you talk."

"I shouldn't have said anything, Bridget. But I know him and he won't give up. It's extremely important that he talk to you. I kind of agree with him." Russell set his tea down then stood.

She watched as he paced the small area she'd sectioned off as her living room. Seeing Russell so upset bothered her. Not because she was worried for herself. She had a knack of keeping herself safe from bad situations—or maybe her guardian angel worked overtime to stop bad things from happening to her.

"I need to talk to Lucercio. He'll know what I should do. Maybe I could leave town or something," she muttered.

Her friend snorted. "Don't run away, Bridget. It'll be fine. Trust me, this man isn't interested in hurting you in any way. To be honest, the scenes that intrigue him are the ones of the garden."

Bridget shot up straight where she sat, gripping her cup so tightly she heard the handle snap off. Luckily she had the saucer underneath it, so there wasn't a spill. Russell rushed over to take the mug from her.

"Did you find him?"

After setting it down on the coffee table, Russell sat on the couch right next to her. He rested his hand on her ankle. She looked into his face, hope springing up in her heart.

"Find who?"

"The man in my dreams," Bridget said.

Russell's chuckle was a little rough around the edges. "I'm not sure he's the man of your dreams."

"I didn't say 'of'. I said 'in my dreams'." Bridget put her hand on Russell's shoulder. "Does he look like the man in those paintings?"

When he hesitated, Bridget shivered in excitement. She couldn't believe that she might be going to get answers to the questions she'd had all of her life.

"He's a dead ringer for that man. Are you sure you've never met him before?"

"Who? Myles?"

Russell reared back, surprise obvious on his face. "You call him Myles?"

She shook her head. "No. He told me to call him Myles during one of my visions. The one in the garden where he's staring up at the sky."

"All right. Well, I guess if you're on first name basis with him, it wouldn't be too bad for you to meet him." Russell bit his bottom lip.

"It's not like we're best friends or anything, Russell. He's just someone I met in a dream." She paused as she thought about how weird that sounded. "Okay, so that didn't sound particularly sane, did it?"

"No, it didn't, but I know what you're talking about. Myles might not be his name," he stated.

She shrugged. "That's what I know him by. I'll keep calling him that until he gives me a different name."

Russell relaxed into the cushions when she smiled at him and she realized he'd been worried that she would freak out about seeing Myles. She leaned over to grab a scone from the plate he'd brought from the kitchen. After taking a bite and swallowing, she pointed it at him.

"Are you going to let him know where I live so we can meet?"

"Hell no. I'm not going to give him your home address or phone number. I don't think he's going to do anything to you, but still, I wouldn't do that for anyone." Russell shot to his feet. "I need something stronger to drink. Do you have anything here?"

"There's a bottle of Merlot in the cabinet. Lucercio brought it over one night when he was in town. Could you bring me another cup?" She jumped to her feet. "Never mind. I need something more to eat than scones and biscuits."

"Sounds good."

They threw together a quick stir-fry and rice. Russell poured himself some wine while she brewed more tea. Once they were at the table, she went back to their conversation.

"I'm willing to meet him. How are we going to do it?"

Russell continued to eat for a little bit and she assumed that he was thinking about it. Bridget stayed quiet, not wanting to push her friend any further. She knew he wasn't thrilled that she'd agreed to it, but she didn't understand why. He'd told her that Myles wasn't dangerous to her.

She knew what that meant. He was a powerful man, probably like Lucercio, which made him dangerous but not someone she needed to be frightened of.

"You'll meet him at the Eye. I want you two where there are other people around. Just to be on the safe side." Russell held up his fork to stop her protest.

"Maybe if you decide to see each other again, he can come here, but not the first time."

"Okay."

His request sounded reasonable and she had been having some good days recently, so she should be able to deal with all those people surrounding her.

"Are you going to call him?"

"He's coming to the gallery tomorrow morning for me to tell him if you'll see him or not. I'll let him know what we set up and call you if he agrees." Russell finished his glass of wine then said, "I'm pretty sure he'll do what we ask."

"Is he handsome?"

He shot her a look but she kept her expression innocent. She had every right to know what the real Myles looked like. Did he look anything like her dreams or had she imagined him as looking better than he did?

"He looks exactly like you painted him. You were very accurate in your depictions."

"He has silver eyes?" She'd never met anyone with eyes that color. Bridget figured that she'd simply made them up when she'd created Myles.

"Yes." Russell took her plate then piled it with his before carrying them to the sink.

"I'll get those, Russell. You don't have to wash my dishes for me."

He waved at her. "Go and paint. Even if you didn't notice your hand twitching, I did. You want to go back to what you were doing before I interrupted you earlier today. That's fine. I'll finish up here then leave. I'll text you after I talk to Myles in the morning."

She jumped to her feet before rushing over to kiss him on the cheek. "Thanks, Russell. You're the best."

"I don't know about that, but you make me plenty of money. I can afford to indulge you once in a while." He flicked a handful of bubbles at her.

Bridget giggled as she went to change into her working clothes, which consisted of a ratty pair of sweats and a ripped T-shirt covered in paint. She twisted her hair up into a messy bun. Ignoring Russell's presence, she put the canvas Lucercio wanted back on the easel and stared at it as she got her paints and brushes ready.

As she fell into the trance state that normally helped her do her artwork, she lost track of time.

At some point, she could feel the fugue state leave her. Russell had left and she'd never even noticed when he'd gone. Bridget washed her brushes, put away her paints, then set the canvas aside so that it could start drying. She didn't want to look at it yet. She would study it in the morning.

After taking a quick shower, she changed into pajamas then slid under the blankets. Curling around her body pillow, she closed her eyes and drifted asleep.

"Bridget, how are you feeling this morning? I heard you had a bad night."

She whirled as Myles approached her from the side of the building. She glanced around to see if any of the attendants were near. There were two of them, but they weren't close enough to interrupt their conversation. In fact, they were smiling at them.

"I'm all right," she said, sliding her hand into the crook of Myles' arm when he offered it to her. "They let me sleep later than usual to make up for it."

He patted her hand as he led her on a slow stroll along one of the garden paths. They wandered through the hedge maze until they were in the clearing. He dusted off a bench with his handkerchief then helped her sit.

"What did you dream about? If you wish to tell me." He placed his hand over his heart. "You know that whatever you share with me will be kept in the strictest confidence."

Bridget nodded as she folded her trembling hands in her lap. She licked her lips as she organized her thoughts. What could she tell him about her dreams? Even she didn't completely understand them.

"There were several winged people dressed in white, but the color could just be me projecting what I think angels would wear."

Myles tilted his head to study her. "Do you think they were angels?"

She shrugged. "What else could they be? They all had wings."

"You have a point," Myles conceded.

His rather easy acceptance of her tales was one of the things she was coming to love about him. He never once acted like he didn't believe her. She appreciated it, even though she knew he was at the County Asylum for the same problems she had. He had visions and heard things that weren't there too.

Yet Myles didn't seem or even act as insane as some of the other people who called the asylum home. Well, it wasn't really home but for her, it wasn't a prison either. She was treated fairly well and was fed. She had her own private room and so far no one had done anything to make her feel uncomfortable or unsafe.

"What were they doing?" He propped his foot on the bench next to her then leaned his elbow on his knee to get closer to her. His silver eyes watched her, never looking away, like she was the center of his world and nothing else mattered.

It was a feeling she'd never had with anyone before. No one acted like they cared about anything she had to say or thought.

"Bridget."

"Sorry. My mind wandered. There were only three of them. One was so beautiful he made me want to cry. Blond hair that almost looked white. His blue eyes were so bright they glowed. If I ever saw him, I would believe he wasn't capable of any kind of wrongdoing. The other two seemed to be arguing with him." She frowned. "I didn't think angels argued."

Myles shrugged. "They might be more like us than we think. Didn't Lucifer get jealous of how much God loved mortals? He believed angels should be higher in God's esteem."

Bridget ran her fingers over the ribbons of her dress while she thought. "I guess that could be true."

She wasn't entirely convinced the story about Lucifer was the entire truth, but what did she know? The stories could all just be lies told to keep people from straying from a good life. She didn't know and never really wanted to speculate about things like that.

"Could you hear what they were saying or was it merely by gestures and expression that you decided they were arguing?" Myles asked.

"Mostly by gestures. The blond kept pointing to something I couldn't see. The other two didn't look convinced by what he was saying." Bridget dared to reach out and touch his arm.

Again Myles covered her hand with his and his smile was soft as he met her gaze. "Is there something you wanted to ask me, Bridget?"

"Do you have someone waiting for you to get out of here?" It was the most subtle way she could ask without coming right out with the question. But a lady didn't ask a gentleman if he had a wife or someone special in his life. Though as she glanced around her, they probably didn't need to stand on ceremony.

His smile broadened and he clasped her hand a little tighter. "No. I have no one special waiting for me. I'm still a *bachelor and assumed I would be for a few years more, but coming here has made me realize I can't wander through life."*

"Have you heard any voices lately? Any whispers on the wind?" She joked a little, but she knew she was the only one who could have a little fun with him.

"Not lately. Whoever wishes to speak to me must be taking some time away from tormenting to bother someone else." He nodded to the bench. "May I sit next to you?"

She nodded, a little nervous because he'd never been that close to her, not even when they walked around the grounds. He kept her hand in his while he shifted to sit, making sure that he wasn't on her dress.

"Why do you suppose they let us be together like this? Most of the others they don't let interact like we do?" Bridget tilted her head in the direction of their attendants.

Myles lifted one of his shoulders in an off-handed shrug. "I'm not sure. Maybe it is because our episodes have never been violent ones. We're no danger to anyone but ourselves. Besides, I think they like the idea of being matchmakers. There probably isn't a lot of happiness in a place like this."

Before she could answer, a buzzing sound filled the air and she looked around, searching for the source. It went on for a little bit then stopped. But before they could continue their conversation, it started again.

"What's that noise?" she asked.

Myles looked at her. "I think you must go, but we will talk some more next time you come back."

"Come back? Where am I going?"

Smiling, he leaned in and whispered, "Open your eyes."

Bridget blinked and discovered that she was staring up at her own ceiling. Another one of those dreams. Only this time, Myles had acted like he knew they were in a different version of their lives. It was almost as though he knew she was dreaming. He'd never reacted that way before.

More buzzing and she realized that it was her phone. After crawling across the bed, she snatched it off the nightstand. It was Russell's number and she remembered that he was going to set up a meeting with the man who'd approached him last night.

Swiping her finger across the screen, she answered, "Hello, Russell."

"Did I wake you?" Russell asked.

"Yes." She rolled onto her back to look up at the ceiling.

He hummed softly, letting her know that he wasn't particularly happy that he had because she didn't get much sleep. "You should've let me leave a voicemail, dear. You need to sleep."

"It's okay, Russell. Did you talk to him?"

"Yes. He'll meet you at the Eye at two this afternoon. I guarantee you'll know him when you see him." He cleared his throat. "Are you sure you don't want me to be there with you?"

She smiled, loving how protective of her he was, and she knew that he had reason to worry. "I'll be fine. If I feel an episode coming on, I'll find a place to sit and call you. Is that all right?"

"It'll have to be." A voice spoke in the background and she could hear Russell reply. When he came back, he said, "I have to go, Bridget. All of your work sold last night, so we've been really busy today."

"I guess I'm glad to hear that." She never knew what to say when Russell told her about the money.

"You should be. Now go back to sleep for a little bit. You have four hours before you have to meet him. Call me when you get home. Love you, dear." Russell ended the call.

She let the phone fall to the mattress as she chose to do as Russell told her. She'd get some more sleep before meeting the man in her dreams.

Chapter Eight

Mika'il paced out of the way of the line for the Eye. Tourists stood there waiting to get into one of the pods on the London landmark, but he wasn't interested in that. He checked his watch and saw that it was only two minutes later than the last time he had looked.

"Why are you pacing like a nervous father?"

Rolling his eyes, Mika'il turned to see Lucifer watching him from where he leaned against the stone wall lining the Thames. *Just what I need.*

"What are you doing here? I would've thought you had a war to start or a coup to encourage." Mika'il hoped that the artist didn't show up while he was chatting with Lucifer. It had annoyed him that Russell hadn't told him the woman's name.

Lucifer chuckled. "Humans don't need my help to do those things. They have always been quite capable of killing each other without invoking my name. Hell, they use the Father as an excuse to end lives as much as they use me."

"And you laugh about it?"

"It's laugh or cry, and I prefer not to be in tears all of my long life. But you didn't answer my question. Why are you so nervous? Are you meeting someone special?" Lucifer eyed him.

Mika'il shook his head. "It's none of your business, Daystar. Go away. You can find me tomorrow and bug me all you want."

Lucifer pushed away from the wall then strolled over to where Mika'il stood. He reached out and almost touched him, but Mika'il stiffened, so Lucifer let his hand drop back to his side. Sadness flashed in Daystar's eyes and Mika'il found himself wishing that he could find a way to forgive the fallen for what he'd done.

He did miss their friendship and the way life had been before the rebellion. Yet he knew they could never go back to the way things had been. They would be dealing with the fallout for eternity.

"I'm leaving. I wouldn't want to contaminate you and whoever you're meeting." Lucifer stopped for a second then continued, "You're a lucky angel, Mika'il. Just keep that in mind. You've done all God has wanted you to do, so you deserve a little happiness."

With another cryptic message, Lucifer disappeared and Mika'il had to take a deep breath to return to his normal calm state. No one—not even William—ever got under Mika'il's skin as fast as Lucifer did. He had a nagging feeling that Lucifer was trying to subtly tell him something, but Mika'il's own anger blocked what the fallen had to say.

"Are you Myles?"

At the familiar, soft-accented voice, Mika'il's heart literally skipped a beat and he froze for a second. *Can it be? Is B Langston the woman I've been searching for?*

Now holding his breath, Mika'il turned around and all became right in his world once more.

"Oh my God. It is you." She gasped then covered her mouth with her hand. Bridget took a step toward him and reached out her other hand to touch his cheek. "I've been dreaming about you my entire life."

"Bridget," was all he could get out before he swept her into his arms then kissed her.

The moment their lips came together, Mika'il thought that the world had stopped around them. He'd been searching through the centuries for the one woman whose very existence had shown him what it meant to be human.

She wound her arms around his neck, pressing as close to him as she could get. He encircled her waist then turned to present his back to the crowd as he relearned her mouth and her taste. Getting lost in her, he forgot where they were.

"I suggest you get a room." Lucifer's voice broke into his thoughts and the shock of it brought Mika'il back to where they were standing.

He stepped back, breaking their kiss but not their embrace. He stared down into her dazed blue eyes and smiled. "I can't believe I've found you."

"Is this real or am I having another vision?" Bridget murmured as she trailed her fingers over the slope of his nose and the curve of his lips.

"It's real, love." He looked around to see if Lucifer was close by. He didn't know why he was worried about the fallen. More than likely, Lucifer had vanished right after making the comment.

There were a few Enforcers and fallen in the crowd of people milling around them, but Lucifer wasn't among them. Mika'il faced Bridget again before he cupped her face.

"Is there somewhere we can go to talk?" He blinked back the tears in his eyes. "I've been searching for you for a long time and I want to hold you without anyone being around."

"Yes. We can go to my place. There's a Tube station nearby. You have a card, right?"

He wanted to tell her that he didn't need an Oyster card, but he wasn't ready to explain who he was and her real identity. She didn't seem to know the truth, and in the middle of a crowd wasn't the right spot to do it.

"Yes. I have one." He stuck his hand in his pocket and willed one into existence. "See?"

Holding it up, he motioned with his head toward the street. Bridget's grin stabbed him in the heart because there was a lot of happiness in it. He remembered when she'd smiled while they'd been at the asylum. There hadn't been a lot of joy in it, though it had grown throughout the months they'd spent together. Almost as if being with him had opened her heart to the possibilities of the world around her.

She took his hand as they made their way past the aquarium to the Westminster Bridge. The day was actually sunny and warmer than it had been lately, so he chose not to flag down a cab. He'd missed strolling with Bridget on his arm, absorbing her presence beside him.

Turning right onto the bridge, they continued to walk without talking, though he could almost hear her wondering how it had happened that they'd found each other. He squeezed her hand and she looked up at him.

"It'll be all right. I'll explain everything when we get to your place. I just hope it makes sense." Mika'il shrugged. "It's complicated and definitely needs you to take a lot on faith."

"You've seen my paintings. You know what I see in visions and dreams. What makes you think I won't believe what you have to tell me?"

"Do you believe in angels?" At her nod, he sighed. "That might make it easier. Do you believe that a soul can continue to return to the world?"

She frowned for a moment while she thought. "You mean like reincarnation?"

He nodded. "Yes."

"But that doesn't make sense," she said as they reached the halfway point on the bridge.

"Why doesn't it?"

"I just never thought about reincarnation in conjunction with angels, is all."

He laughed, but he wasn't entirely sure how he could explain how her life had gone without using reincarnation. Some of the memories in her head were of parents that she'd had at one time. Yet at what time in her life had they disappeared? Was it when she was young and before the asylum? Did she think she'd been born only thirty-five years ago or did she have an inkling that she'd been around for far longer than that?

Mika'il wasn't sure what the answers to any of those questions were, and wouldn't until they got somewhere he could ask them without being interrupted.

"I love this city." Stopping, Bridget turned to look up at Big Ben. "There's so much history on every street and there are moments when I feel like I've lived here in different times. Watched this town grow into what it is now."

He glanced around as his memories of a Regency London overlapped the twenty-first century city. He had watched London evolve until he'd lost Bridget then he'd refused to come and see what it looked like.

He gathered her closer. "I'm so glad I went to that gallery last night. If I hadn't, I probably wouldn't have ever found you again."

"How did you lose me? And when did we meet?" Bridget giggled. "Aside from my dreams, and we were dressed differently then."

"That's true."

They'd reached the Westminster Tube station, so they took the steps down and he checked the map.

"Where are we headed?"

"Regent's Street. My place is a few streets from there."

Looking at the map again, he sighed. "I wished I had asked you before this. There's a stop close to the Embankment that would've been a straighter shot for us to your stop."

"Doesn't matter. What's a little longer ride?" She didn't seem bothered by the thought of being surrounded by people.

Mika'il wished that he could act as nonchalantly. For as much time as he had spent among mortals, he'd never gotten used to being with them. No matter how hard he tried, he couldn't always block out their thoughts and some of them were very disturbed individuals.

They scanned their cards then made their way to the right platform. She settled against his side and he ran his hand up and down her arm as they waited for the train. He glanced at her, noticing that her eyes were closed while her lips moved like she was talking to herself. He smiled slightly as he leaned down to whisper in her ear.

"To whom are you talking?"

She didn't open her eyes. "I'm trying not to sink into my head and ignore the people around us."

"I thought you didn't mind being on the Tube with everyone," he reminded her.

"I thought it would be okay, but I'm finding that I've reached my limit of dealing with the crush of humanity."

Sweat popped out on her brow, causing him to bring her closer. "I didn't realize you had problems with being out in public."

"I don't always, but after being out last night for the gallery opening, I might have overestimated my tolerance level today." She paled.

Looking around, he found a spot where he could tuck them away from everyone. He wrapped his arms around her waist then brought her into his chest as he moved them to where they could hide out.

"Do you trust me?" He grinned when she looked up at him. "I know it might be too soon to ask you that, but really? Do you trust me?"

"I wouldn't let you kiss me or take you home if I didn't." She rolled her eyes. "Why?"

"I can get us to your place without having to ride the Tube and be around anyone else." He had planned on telling her the truth when he got them back home, but he wasn't sure she'd be quite as open-minded as she seemed.

"All right." She closed her eyes again before pressing her face into his shirt.

"Think about your flat and what it looks like," Mika'il told her.

He slowly slipped into her mind, caught the images of her home before pulling back out. He wasn't going to rummage around in the rest of her thoughts. Once he had the place fixed in his head, he gathered his power then let it go.

When his vision cleared and he felt his body again, he opened his eyes. They were standing in the middle of a studio style flat. It had to be Bridget's because he could smell a hint of turpentine and oil paint.

Stepping away from her, he said, "Bridget, we're here."

She blinked once before glancing around to discover that they were in the middle of her living room. "How did you get us here?"

Mika'il grimaced. "It's a long story and I'm willing to tell it to you, but first maybe you'd like to change into something more comfortable. I can make us some tea while you do so."

Bridget stared at him for a moment before she held out her hand. "Come with me."

"Honey, we need to talk first."

"No. We've been together before, haven't we?" She moved closer.

"Not as close as we could've been," he admitted, taking her hand in his. "It was a different era and I didn't want to take advantage of you, Bridget."

"So all those dreams I've had about you were real?"

He shrugged. "I don't know what they all were, but I would think most of them were."

"Then we can talk later."

Mika'il let her tug him over to where tri-fold panel screens partitioned off her bed from the rest of the room. He didn't protest when she shoved his coat off his shoulders and allowed it to fall to the floor.

"Are you sure?"

As much as he'd been hoping to find her again and get to this point, he didn't want to do anything that she might regret. Mika'il knew he'd never feel bad about taking her to bed.

Bridget stopped then put her hands on his face to make sure his gaze met hers. "I'm sure that I want you to make love to me, Myles. I've been dreaming about you for all of my life. Hell, I've must have loved you when we knew each other all those centuries ago. I've been waiting for you to find me and I'm not going to let you walk away from me."

Mika'il encircled her waist with his arm then pulled her against his body. He crushed their lips together and she gasped. He swept his tongue in as she opened to him. Not wanting to rush, he held her, simply kissing her then trailing his mouth over her jaw and down her throat to the soft triangle at the base.

He sucked on her soft skin for a second before easing her away. Staring down into her dazed blue eyes, he couldn't believe he'd somehow managed to find her after all those centuries.

After wrapping his fingers in the hem of her shirt, he tugged it up over her head. He let it drop from his hands as he stared at her. A white lace and cotton bra covered small but perfect breasts. Her lightly tanned skin glowed. He reached out to brush the tips of his fingers over the curve of her breast, causing her to shiver.

Mika'il picked her up then laid her on the bed. Once he'd done that, he stripped her jeans off and saw that she wore matching panties. He placed one knee on the mattress before tracing a line from between her breasts down over her belly to the waistband of her underwear. She sucked her stomach in as though she was encouraging him to continue. Bridget stroked along his shoulder as he smiled at her.

He leaned down to lick along the edge of her bra, dipping his tongue under the lace to tease her nipple. While he did that, he managed to get his hand under her back to unhook her bra. After helping her take it off, he nuzzled each nipple before settling his mouth over one.

"Oh my," she whispered as he pinched the flesh between his teeth then tugged it.

Chapter Nine

Bridget arched, the slight twinge of pain shooting through her like electricity. She couldn't remember ever having had such a reaction to a man before. Maybe it had to do with him having been in her mind all of her life, however long that life had been.

Russell would be having a fit when he heard that she'd brought Myles home and he'd probably lose his mind if he ever found out that she'd slept with him after having met him an hour ago. Yet again, it was like she'd known him all her life. He wasn't some stranger she'd just met.

They had spent more time talking with each other than she'd ever actually done with any of her other lovers. Who cared that their conversations had been in her dreams. None of that mattered. All that mattered was that Myles was in her arms and bed… Finally.

"Myles," she pleaded.

He eased away to look at her and she met his silver gaze. "My name is Mika'il, Bridget. Not Myles."

"Mika'il," she murmured. She threaded her fingers through his hair to pull him back to her.

When he covered her with his body, she moaned as the fabric of his shirt rubbed over her nipples. He slipped his fingers under her panties and she shuddered when he brushed them over her clit before he stripped the underwear from her.

He settled between her thighs, keeping her legs spread. She moaned as he blew a puff of air over her heated flesh. She almost levitated when he swiped his tongue along her pussy. He pressed one of his fingers inside her then two.

"Please," she begged then he surged up to suck her nipples while thrusting in and out of her. Using his thumb, he played with her clit to build her excitement.

She gripped his biceps as she rocked in rhythm with his touches. Her pleasure grew and grew until all she could think about was falling from the cliff into the sea of desire. Just before she did, Mika'il eased away from her.

"Mika'il, no," she protested.

"Hush, honey. I'm just undressing. I want to be inside you when you come," he said.

Bridget rolled onto her side to watch as he quickly undressed. Removing his clothes revealed a body of solid muscle covered by golden skin. His chest was covered with a light dusting of darker blond hair that spread from nipple to nipple then in a thin line down to his groin.

His cock rose from the curls at its base and she couldn't help reaching out for it. Mika'il didn't stop her as she wrapped her hand around his shaft then pumped. His moan brought her gaze up to his burning one.

"Do you have a condom?"

In the time it took her to blink, a condom was being held out to her. She didn't question where it had come from. Just like she'd never questioned how they'd gone from the Westminster platform to her flat in a single breath. It wasn't important to her at the moment. All she wanted was to feel him on top of her, thrusting into her and bringing them both to climax.

Bridget took the foil packet from him before tearing it open. After getting it out, she rolled it on him then took him in her mouth for a quick suck. But when he would've pushed in again, she backed off, though she kept her hold on him, leading him back to the bed by his cock.

They settled back on the bed and Bridget welcomed him into her body. As he slid into her wet pussy, she sighed, loving the way he filled her. Once Mika'il was buried as deep inside as he could get, he paused and stared down at her.

"Love me," she whispered.

His silver gaze flared with need and emotion. "Always, Bridget."

Bridget grinned as she ordered, "Then fuck me."

She wrapped her arms around him as he braced one of his hands on the bed next to her head. He started thrusting and she moved with him. Sliding his other hand down, he teased her clit as well, driving her back into a fevered level of passion and desire.

"Oh my!" she cried as she orgasmed, pleasure washing over her in waves.

Mika'il shouted out her name as he slammed into her then froze as he came. Panting, he jerked slightly until he collapsed on top of her for a few minutes while he caught his breath. She ran her hands up and down his sweaty back, not caring that he was mashing her into the mattress.

Finally, he held onto the rubber as he pulled out. Bridget saw him wander down to her bathroom.

While he was gone, she got up to tug the covers down before she climbed under them.

She heard the toilet flush then water run. Curling around one of her pillows, she took a deep breath as her eyes drifted shut. The mattress dipped behind her and she smiled when he wrapped his arm around her waist to pull her close.

"We'll take a short nap then we'll talk about what's going on between us," he murmured in her ear then kissed the nape of her neck.

"All right."

Bridget fell asleep, listening to Mika'il breathing and feeling content for the first time in her life.

* * * *

The buzzing of a phone woke her later on. She lay in her bed, trying to figure out who was with her. She didn't bring men home to her flat, yet there was a man in bed with her. The buzzing started up again.

"Are you going to answer that?" The question came from behind her.

Myles—or Mika'il as he'd told her his name was. The guy who'd starred in all of her dreams and visions was holding her in his arms while they were naked. She ached a little bit, so they'd done more than just sleep. With that thought, all the events of the last couple of hours came back to her and she sighed.

"I probably should. It'll be Russell checking up on me," she said as she crawled out of bed to pad out to the living room where she'd left her phone in her bag.

It had stopped ringing by the time she got it out, but she scrolled through to Russell's number and hit the dial button.

"Are you all right?" Russell asked as he answered.

"I'm fine, Russell. I just didn't have my phone nearby. It took me a minute to get to it."

She heard the bed squeak and she glanced over to see Mika'il walk around the screen panels. God, the man shouldn't ever be allowed to walk around naked. Women would be tripping over themselves if they got to see him without clothes.

That's not going to happen ever. Bridget wasn't going to let any other female see Mika'il like that. No other girl would share his bed ever again.

"Bridget. Bridget!"

"What?" She tore her gaze away from Mika'il, but not before she had caught his smug expression.

"I was asking if you met Myles and how did it go?" Russell sounded exasperated.

Bridget laughed. "You mean Mika'il?"

Russell inhaled sharply. "He told you his real name?"

"His real name? Have you met Mika'il before, Russell? And if you had, why didn't you tell me about him?" She sat on her couch as she asked.

"No. I hadn't met him before the other night, but I knew who he was. I'd never seen his face, so I couldn't know that the man you painted and talked about was him," Russell protested. "It wasn't until I saw him that I realized that Myles and Mika'il were the same. I don't hang around his crowd of people."

"His crowd of people?"

Mika'il turned to look at her from where he stood in her kitchen, his eyebrows raised in a silent question. Bridget noticed that he'd put some water on for tea. They were going to be talking as soon as she had ended her conversation with Russell. *We're going to have to get dressed. There's no way I'll be able to keep my hands off him.*

"Aside from him telling you his name, have you done any other talking?" Suspicion colored Russell's voice.

Her face heated as she blushed. "Umm…"

"Oh, Bridget, you didn't sleep with him, did you?"

She could hear his concern in his inquiry. "What would you like to hear, Russell? Do you want me to lie to you or just tell you the truth?" She rolled her eyes and Mika'il laughed.

"You don't know him, honey. I don't think getting that involved with him is a good idea."

"Russell, I've been over this with you. I've dreamt of Mika'il for years and something tells me those dreams were memories. I looked into his eyes and I knew his heart."

Mika'il strolled over to her then dropped next to her on the couch. He took her hand in his before lifting it to his mouth, kissing her knuckles. She smiled but he didn't stick around. He went on back to the bedroom and she heard the rustle of fabric. He was either making the bed or getting dressed.

Her friend sighed. "I'm sorry, Bridget. I'm just afraid you're going to get hurt." Before she could say anything, though, he continued, "But you know your own mind, I guess, and I'll be here for you if you need me. If he'll let me close to you after this."

"Why wouldn't he let you see me?" She frowned.

"Maybe I'll explain some day. I'll let you go, but talk to him. There's a lot you need to discover about Mika'il and his world. Call me tomorrow to let me know that you're okay." Russell hung up.

She set her phone on the coffee table and stared in the direction of her bed. Dressed, Mika'il walked over to her, holding her robe in his hand. Bridget took it from him to slip it on.

"Do you want something to eat with your tea?" Mika'il asked before wandering back over to the stove to get the boiling water off.

"Sure."

Sitting there, she watched as he prepared a tray with teapot, cups, milk and sugar. He also put together some sandwiches, crackers and cheese then brought the whole thing over to her. After setting it down, he poured out her cup, adding just the right amount of milk and sugar.

"Have we had tea before?" She took her cup from him.

"Why do you ask?" He leaned back into the corner of the couch while studying her.

"Because you didn't ask me how I wanted my tea. You just did it and handed it to me."

He blinked and smiled. "Did I get it right?"

Bridget took a sip then nodded. "Perfect. What would you like to eat?" She gestured toward the food.

Mika'il shook his head. "No. Help yourself."

Not interested in food, she organized her thoughts. Once she had gotten them in order, she pursed her lips. *How do I start the conversation?* It wasn't as though she was afraid of what Mika'il had to say to her. She'd already accepted, long before she knew he was real, that she was painting scenes from a former life.

"When did we know each other?"

Mika'il pinched his bottom lip between his thumb and finger while he seemed to be deciding what to say.

"You've seen the artwork at the showing. I painted us in a garden with a fountain. Was I right about that?"

"Yes. It was the County Asylum of Northumberland and we met in the spring of eighteen hundred and sixteen." He turned the cup round and round on the saucer. "We were both patients there for having visions and hearing voices."

"That explains a lot," she muttered.

"What do you mean?"

Bridget motioned toward the canvases leaning up against various walls. "I've always painted those scenes, never really understanding what they meant, but somehow knowing they were part of my past. Are you saying I've been reborn?"

Shrugging, Mika'il frowned. "I'm not sure exactly how it works for you. I'm not sure if you're being reborn or if you simply have lived all those years and the only way you can deal with it is by creating new lives for yourself in your mind."

She ran through everything. The only memories she had were vague images of a man and a woman she'd always assumed were her parents. Yet had they been? And if they were, what had happened to her?

"To be honest, the only person I remember being around since I first started remembering things is Lucercio. I only asked him about my parents once and he said they died when I was young, but he'd been friends with them, so he'd kept an eye on me." She snorted. "Not a very good eye, admittedly. I left the foster system when I was eighteen, then lived on the streets because of the visions and voices. I couldn't function at times."

Setting the cup and saucer down, she clasped her hands together. "I still have my moments when I have episodes and I'll wander away from here. I'll be wandering the streets for days until the fugue goes away then I'll return."

Mika'il eased closer before taking her hands in his. "I'm sorry about those. It has to be hard."

"It is, but I got used to them. Plus Lucercio would help me find my way back. I hear him in my head at times," she confessed.

He tilted his head to stare at her, yet she didn't get the feeling that he thought she was crazy for thinking that. "Have you seen him along with hearing him?"

"Oh yes, and Russell has seen him as well. He isn't a figment of my imagination," she insisted.

"I believe you." He squeezed her hands and smiled. "What if I told you all of that is reasonable considering who you are?"

"Who I am?" Bridget eyed him. "I'm just me. No one special, in spite of my ability to paint."

Mika'il took a deep breath before he said, "You're an angel."

Chapter Ten

Mika'il waited to see how Bridget would react to his statement. She looked deep into his eyes and he did his best to portray his sincerity. Then she laughed.

"I'm glad you think I'm an angel, Mika'il, but that doesn't explain anything." She tugged to try to get her hands free.

"No. I'm serious, Bridget. You're an angel. A true, honest-to-God, heavenly angel." Mika'il let her go before standing. "I'm Mika'il, the archangel. Not Myles."

"Right." She didn't look convinced.

Gathering his power to him, Mika'il let the illusion he wore drop. His wings exploded from his shoulders, towering over his head before cascading down to the floor. He could see his glowing reflection in her eyes. Power almost seemed to drip from him onto the floor and swirled around his feet.

"Holy cow!" Bridget stared at him with wide eyes. "You're serious."

"Yes." He unfurled his wings, flapping them slightly to create enough of a breeze that her hair fluttered in it. "I hide my true nature because mortals have a problem believing what they see."

"I've painted you like this. I must have seen you at some time." She jumped to her feet and before he could grab her, she dashed across the flat to where several canvases were propped against a brick wall.

He hid his wings and glow again before following her. As he approached her, she pulled a large square out from under six other ones. When Bridget turned it around, his jaw dropped. She really had captured him in his angelic glory, with wings and glow. Also, she'd added the sword that he'd used during the rebellion.

"How did you do that? I don't remember you being around when the rebellion happened." He snapped his mouth shut after saying that.

"I wasn't around when the rebellion happened? Where was I?"

Mika'il took her hand to drag her back to the couch. He dropped down on the cushions then pulled her right next to him. He kept his arm around her and she didn't argue.

"Well, here's the thing. It's really not going to make much sense because it doesn't to me. Of course, I don't ask too many questions, but it seems that at some point before Lucifer and the others fell, God allowed a group of angels to go to live among the mortals." He grimaced as he thought about how to explain it. "This group consisted of twenty angels, but unfortunately, he lost touch with them."

"How can God lose touch with his angels? I don't understand." She wrinkled her nose.

"I know. I think what happened isn't so much that he lost touch with them, but that they lost their connection with him. They slowly became more human and so over the years, the angels forgot they were angels."

"But did we die like mortals or not?" Bridget asked.

"God tasked me with the job of finding the lost ones and I did find twelve of them rather quickly, so they never had to die to find that out. Six of the remaining eight did die and began their true mortal lives. Yet their souls were reborn each time and they blended even more into mortal lives. It was very hard to track them down once that happened."

He closed his eyes and pictured his group of friends hanging together at Dominic's club along with Cassandra and Nevan in Los Angeles. It had taken him time to find them, but he'd discovered where they were then hooked them up with fallen, bringing each one of them back to heaven. It was one of the things that made his job worth doing.

"What about the other two?"

He shrugged one shoulder. "There is one still missing. You seem to have stayed the closest to an angel. Your visions and dreams are memories of things you did as an angel in Heaven. You remember me from those moments and from our meeting in Northumberland. I was spending some time as a mortal and fell in love with you. Then when I returned to Heaven to take my job back, I lost you again. You disappeared and I couldn't find a trace of you anywhere."

"How did that happen?" She looked unconvinced.

"I have no idea. I'm not infallible, my love. I do make mistakes. Heck, I feel like I've made a hundred mistakes when it comes to Lucifer," he muttered, but he shook that off to continue with their conversation. "Do you remember anything after our time together?"

She bit her bottom lip as she thought. "No. I don't. All I know about is when we met and that's it. After that, the only memories in my head are from the time I left foster care and Lucercio found me in an alleyway."

"I don't know if we'll ever find out what happened to you after I left. I'm just glad that you're safe and I found you." He pulled Bridget into his arms and kissed her, unable to resist touching her.

Wrapping her arms around his shoulders, she leaned back until she was flat on the couch and he lay on top of her. He fumbled with the belt on her robe, but got it open so that he could cup her breasts. She moaned when Mika'il rubbed his thumbs over her nipples.

Mika'il kissed along her jaw down her neck to her chest where he suckled on one of the hard bits of flesh. Bridget buried her fingers in his hair, not letting him move away from her. But when he tried to move further down her body, she tugged on his ear.

Pushing up, he looked down at her and she grinned. "Let's go back to bed. It'll be comfortable and I can have a little fun as well."

He was more than willing to do that, so he scooped her into his arms before carrying her to the other part of the flat. She burst out laughing when he tossed her into the middle of the mattress then followed her down. She placed her hand on his chest while shaking her head.

"We both need to be naked," she told him.

"You're right." Mika'il stripped first her then him and crawled onto the bed afterwards. "So, you call the shots. What should we do now?"

"I think you need to swing your ass over here, so I can suck you."

All his blood headed south and he was instantly aching with lust. To feel her lush lips around his cock had been a fantasy he had only let out in his deepest thoughts and he'd never dreamt that it would happen. He shifted around until the head of his dick brushed her lips and he found himself facing her pussy.

She had just a small patch of pubic hair with the rest of her vagina being bare. He pulled her soft, wet lips apart to reveal her clit and as he flicked it with his tongue, she sucked his length down.

He used his tongue, teeth and fingers to pleasure her and he barely managed not to shove his shaft into her mouth and choke her as she blew him. It was the type of mutual building of desire that he'd always wanted to indulge in, but hadn't ever been able to do once he'd lost her.

Bridget teased her fingers along his balls and the soft patch of skin right behind them. She pumped his cock with her hand in rhythm to bobbing her head up and down the length of it. He felt his balls draw close to his body, but he didn't want to come in her mouth.

He stopped and she let him slide from her mouth as he rolled off her. Flipping around, he looked at her.

"I want to spill my seed inside you," he announced and she grew thoughtful.

"What about babies?"

"You can't have any. As an angel, even a lost one, you can't have children. I'm sorry if that disappoints you." He cradled her face with his hands. "I probably should've told you that in a nicer way."

"No. It's all right. I'm not sure I'd be a good mother anyway, given all my problems. At least I know I'm not crazy now, and it all had been real at one point or another." She stroked her fingers over his chest to press them against his heart. "I love you, my archangel. I want to feel you inside me without anything between us."

He flopped over onto his back, taking her with him, and encouraged her to straddle his hips. Holding his cock in position, he helped to balance her while she slowly impaled herself on him.

Her warm heat enveloped him and his groan joined hers. Bridget braced her hands on his chest while lifting herself up then letting her body fall back on his shaft. He allowed her to control the pace of their lovemaking for a little while, wanting her to get adjusted to having him inside her.

When he thought she was ready and he just couldn't take it anymore, he grabbed her waist and planted his feet on the mattress before starting to thrust up when she came down.

"Mika'il," she cried out as he kept speeding up.

"Touch yourself," he commanded and she slipped one of her hands between her thighs to rub her clit.

He jerked once when he felt her fingertips brush against his heated flesh as he stroked in and out. Pressure began building in his groin and he knew he was close.

"Bridget love, I want you to come with me," he told her.

She bit her lip and nodded, but he could tell she needed something more. With a heave of his muscles, he flipped them over again so that she was on her back now. She changed the angle of her hips, causing him to drive even deeper into her. He bent then bit her shoulder and she screamed as she came.

Her inner muscles milked his length, contracting and loosening in a rhythm that drove him over the edge. His climax hit him like a truck and he flooded her with his cum. Mika'il continued to rock inside her until he thought that every last bit of his soul had left his body and entered hers.

With an exhausted moan, he collapsed, having just enough sense to move to one side so that he didn't smother her with his weight. She winced slightly as his softening cock slid out.

"Are you okay?" he asked in between gulps of air while he tried to calm his breathing.

Nodding, she snuggled against him, laying her head on his shoulder. He encircled her shoulders to bring her closer.

"Does this mean we get to be together now? That I'll go back to Heaven with you and all that?" she asked.

"I'm not entirely sure how it'll work, but I do know that I won't be letting you go. If it comes down to it, I'll give up my place in Heaven to come down and be with you until you die." He knew it was the only real choice he had.

Mika'il wasn't going to risk losing the woman he loved just to go back to Heaven to be *the* archangel again. A warm sensation blossomed in his chest and he realized that God wasn't going to make him choose between him and Bridget.

"She'll come back to Heaven with you. There has always been a place waiting for her."

"I guess you'll be coming back with me when we're ready," he informed Bridget.

"Will I be allowed to keep painting? What about Russell?"

He laughed softly. "I'm sure you can paint. We do get some downtime where the mortal world is calm for a minute or two. As for Russell, try not to worry about him. He's a true demon and they've been around since the world was created. He'll land on his feet."

"A true demon? Does that mean he's evil?" She met his gaze with her own worried one.

"Not necessarily. True demons can be good or evil. Most of them are more neutral. They are simply out for what they can gain. Some go getting that by hurting people. Others go about earning it like mortals would, and it seems like Russell is that kind of demon." He smoothed his hand down her spine.

"I want you to meet Lucercio before we go," she announced.

"And I want you to meet the other six lost angels, though you can't say anything to them about who they truly are. They don't realize their true calling yet."

"I won't," she promised.

Mika'il hugged her close then pressed a kiss on her brow. "We should get some sleep then we can meet your guardian angel tomorrow, if he's in town."

"Oh he is. He stopped by before I left for the showing the other night. I'll call him tomorrow and set up a time for us to get together."

As he was drifting off, he felt as though someone was watching them. He pushed his power out into the flat to see if he could sense anyone else's presence, but there was nothing. *Just a false alarm.* He settled Bridget closer to him and slid into a deep sleep like he'd never experienced before.

Lucifer stood, hidden by his own considerable power in the corner of the flat. He stared at Mika'il and Bridget lying in her bed. With a wave of his hand, he covered them with the comforter so that neither of them would get cold.

Happiness warred with sadness in his heart at the thought of Bridget and Mika'il finally being able to be together. It was good to see Mika'il content for once and Bridget joyful at the knowledge that she wasn't crazy, even though he'd tried to tell her that for as long as he'd been watching out for her.

The sadness that was a normal part of his everyday makeup swelled at the idea of never having Bridget to talk to again. Once she returned to Heaven, she wouldn't be leaving it, especially not for the worst of the fallen angels. Something wet dripped on his hand and Lucifer reached up to touch his cheek. Was he crying?

That wasn't possible, considering that he'd gotten into this entire mess of his own accord. He had nothing to cry or mourn anymore. It was simply him against the world and Heaven. He'd learnt how to deal with loneliness, but he could confess to himself — if no one else — that he was tired.

Bridget muttered in her sleep and Lucifer sent out a small tendril of power to touch her cheek in a silent benediction. He would meet them tomorrow and face Mika'il's wrath once more before saying goodbye to them both for good.

Chapter Eleven

"All right. We'll meet you in front of the National Portrait Gallery at Trafalgar Square in an hour," Bridget said, glancing at Mika'il to make sure that the time was okay.

He nodded, intrigued by what she'd told him about Lucercio. The man had found her in an alleyway and brought her to the flat that she lived in now. He'd shown her that she could paint by buying her supplies and challenging her to paint him a picture. Once she had, and he'd seen how remarkable it was, he'd found her an agent in Russell. Bridget had explained that Lucercio talked to her in her mind and always helped her find her way back from the trances she got lost in, or when she wandered too far from home.

Mika'il wanted to tell the man thank you for watching over Bridget. What kind of man would help her out and not expect anything in return for his support? He needed to ask Lucercio why.

"See you soon." She hung up then walked over to give Mika'il a kiss. "Are you ready to go?"

"We don't need to leave yet. I can just pop us over there when we need to be there," he told her once they'd broken apart.

Bridget giggled. "While I love the idea of not having to deal with the crowds of people on the Tube, I think I'd like to travel like a normal person does until it's time for us to leave."

"Fine then. Let's head out. If we get there early, we can wander around for a while." He created an overcoat for himself out of thin air, causing her to gasp. "Sorry, but it looks a little cool out and I didn't exactly pack an overnight bag."

"I know, but it's still a little strange that you can do that, even though I believe you're an angel." She went to her armoire to dig out a jacket for herself.

When they were ready to go, he escorted her out of her flat, locking the door behind them. He ensured that they didn't rush to get to the Tube station because he liked strolling along on the busy London pavement.

"What does Lucercio look like?" he questioned as they went through the turnstiles before making their way to the right platform.

"Trust me. You'll know which one he is when we get there. He has a habit of standing out in a crowd, though I don't think he even notices that he does so." Bridget frowned. "He's a very lonely, sad man at times, but I know he'd be terribly upset if he realized I knew that about him."

"What do you really know about him?" He escorted her onto one of the trains before letting her choose their seats.

They settled in and she held his hand while she thought and smiled. "Not much. He's never talked about himself the entire time we've known each other.

It's always been about me. I'm afraid I'm not a very good friend to him."

"Do you think he would accept help or care from you?"

"No." Her answer was swift and sure. "He would hate even the thought of me asking him that."

Mika'il urged her a little closer to him then brought his lips close to her ear. "Is he going to be upset that you're in love with someone else?"

The look she shot him held shock and confusion. "No. Why would he?"

"I thought he might be in love with you and he'd be jealous of our relationship." He shrugged.

She giggled. "Oh, wait until you meet him and you'll understand why that is a ridiculous question."

"Okay, honey. I'll reserve all judgment until I meet this Lucercio face to face."

They spent the rest of their travel across the city talking about Bridget's life and some of the things Mika'il had done in the millennia he'd been around. He also let her know that they were going to Dominic's nightclub later on to celebrate its grand opening with the others.

He helped her to stand when they got off at their stop for Trafalgar Square, offering his arm to her once they had gotten to the street level. The day had dawned bright and clear, and while it was a bit cool at the moment, he knew it was going to be warmer later on. All in all, a beautiful London day to spend with the woman he loved.

"There he is."

Mika'il glanced in the direction Bridget was waving and he stopped in his tracks as he watched Bridget race over to hug Lucifer. *It can't be. How can Lucifer be the one who watched over Bridget all those centuries? It* wasn't in the fallen's character to take care of others. All he really cared about was himself.

"Mika'il, come over and meet my very own guardian angel," Bridget called to him.

Lucifer smirked over her head at Mika'il who wanted to smack that smug expression off his face.

"It's nice to finally meet the man of her dreams," Lucifer said when Mika'il had approached them.

Mika'il forced himself to shake hands with the fallen then glanced at Bridget. "Would you give us a few moments alone?"

She shot a glance between them and must have sensed the tension because she didn't argue. "I'll just go over to the fountain." Her actions suited her words.

They both stood there for a moment, watching as she walked away. Then Mika'il whirled on Lucifer.

"You knew who she was? How is that possible? I never sensed you close to me in all those years." Mika'il frowned as he tried to remember any instant of uneasiness that might have clued him in to Lucifer's presence.

"You were mortal, Mika'il. Of course you wouldn't have been able to sense me. I might have fallen, but I still have the power to hide myself from the humans I live among." Lucifer shot an annoyed look at the people walking around them. "Mortals—even those who used to be archangels—aren't perceptive enough to feel me if I don't want them to."

"Are you the reason why I couldn't find her when I went back? Had you taken her?"

Mika'il turned to see Bridget standing near the fountain and staring up at the statue of Lord Nelson at the very top of the pillar. The pull to go to her and wrap his arms around her surprised him. It wasn't a possessive urge. It was more protective, as though he worried that she'd disappear on him again.

"Yes."

He whirled to glare at Lucifer. "Why would you do that to me? Do you hate me that much that you would hide the woman I love away from me? Did you enjoy seeing me suffer?"

Lucifer's dark eyes narrowed and grew cold. "I've never liked seeing you suffer or hurt. Unlike you, who seem to always revel in anything that brings me pain. I didn't hurt you when I fell. I turned my back on God, but not on you, and yet you took it personally." Lucifer clenched his hands by his sides. "You've welcomed all of those who asked for forgiveness back into your good graces, even if they are still forbidden Heaven. Yet you still treat me like a pariah. Why?"

Mika'il took a deep breath as he allowed Lucifer's agonized question to ring in his ears. His former friend was right. While he'd wept for all the ones Lucifer had led astray, he'd never once shed a tear for Lucifer. He'd never once considered forgiving Daystar for the actions that had destroyed so many that day.

"Because you've never shown remorse for what happened. If just once you asked forgiveness or explained why you did it, I might be able to thaw my heart toward you. Yet you've never tried to explain when I asked. You joke and evade, but you never say anything worth hearing." Anger caused Mika'il's skin to heat as he thought about all the fallen whose wings he'd taken and heard again their cries of agony when they were denied Heaven.

"You need to listen more closely, Mika'il. Many things I've said to you are worth listening to, but you've shut your ears to me." Lucifer motioned toward Bridget. "I hid her away from you and the world until she was strong enough to survive on her own. Then I placed her where you would be able to discover her."

Mika'il blinked as the thought that Lucifer might have set this whole thing up struck him. "Are you saying you planned for all of this? That you knew I'd be coming to London and you set it up so that Bridget would be here as well?"

"I merely put the ball in play. What happened after that was none of my concern." Lucifer shot Mika'il a smug grin. "But it turned out rather well, don't you think?"

He wanted to grab the fallen and shake him as hard as he could. "See, this is why I have a hard time believing you. There is nothing humble about you."

"The humble man has no pain to hide. The arrogant man has an entire lifetime of agony to disguise." Lucifer glanced over at Bridget. "I kept her safe for you because I knew you loved her."

Mika'il almost missed what he had said because he was looking away from him.

"Why would you do that? Why do something like that when I've been a jerk to you for centuries and I might never have found out what you did?" Disbelief rocked through Mika'il.

"You finding out never mattered to me. What mattered most was you being happy. Both of you being able to love, and Bridget being able to return home. She survived because I kept an eye on her. Watching her deal with the visions and memories hurt me far more than losing Heaven did." Lucifer swallowed, but didn't say anything else.

"You know who she is?" Mika'il couldn't believe that Lucifer would know about the mission God had given to Mika'il from the moment the other angels fell.

"I know exactly who she is. You aren't the only one he talks to, Mika'il."

And with that bombshell, Lucifer disappeared. Mika'il stared at the space where the fallen had been standing. God still spoke to Lucifer? How was that possible? Hadn't he been banished from God's presence when he rebelled?

Mika'il's head hurt as he tried to process all the questions now racing through his head. Bridget approached him from where she'd been standing next to one of the lion statues in Trafalgar Square. He held out his hand and she took it then smiled at him.

"Are you done with your meeting? Where did Lucercio go? Why didn't he say goodbye?"

"He told me to tell you goodbye for him."

"Lucercio looked sad. Well, sadder than usual." Bridget frowned as she looked up at him. "What did you argue about?"

Mika'il shook his head. "What do you mean, sadder than usual?"

She nodded. "I told you he seemed lonely and sad, but this time it was like he was losing his best friend or something. I've never seen him so heartbroken."

"Really? Has he ever done anything to you?" He tucked her hand in the crook of his elbow as they strolled around the square then headed toward The Mall and Buckingham Palace.

"No. Why would he? He's done things for me, like kept me from freaking out when visions overtook me. If I couldn't stop them, he protected me from people who would've taken advantage of me while I was in the throes of those visions." Bridget hugged his arm close to her.

Mika'il didn't plan on going all the way to the Palace, but the weather was nice for a change and he wanted to spend time with Bridget outside so that they could talk. They tended to get distracted when they were alone inside. Of course, she distracted him when she smiled or laughed or walked.

"But he's never hurt you?"

She stopped to look at him. "Why would he do that, Mika'il? He never hurt or lied to me. All Lucercio has done is keep me safe and I don't know why. It had to take a lot of time to do what he did for me."

Shrugging, he patted her hand. "I think he did it so you and I could find each other again, Bridget. He wanted to make sure you stayed alive long enough for me to come back here."

"Why didn't you come back before this? Was what we had so terrible that you wanted to forget?" Bridget wrinkled her forehead in thought. "Wait. We knew each other a long time ago, didn't we? I mean like hundreds of years ago, right? I didn't think we lived that long."

"Mortals don't live that long, Bridget, but you aren't mortal. You do remember that, right?" He didn't want to upset her, but he needed her to accept what her reality was. They had gone over it all the day before. Of course, they'd gone on to make love again, so he wasn't sure how much she remembered after getting distracted like that.

Tilting her head, she narrowed her eyes as she stared down the street. When she pursed her lips and nodded, he felt a rush of relief. There were times when he knew she didn't remember things that had happened throughout the millennia she had lived. He should be happy that she didn't seem to have a problem remembering him.

"I'm an angel, right? One that God lost track of for some reason," she said.

"Right. He's never explained how it happened, but you are one of them. That's why you had all those memories of Heaven and who you used to be." He encircled her waist then pulled her close to him. He brushed a kiss over the top of her head as they continued along the way, dodging tourists and city dwellers making their way to offices or tourist destinations.

"Who is Lucercio then? If he isn't an angel like you and me, and he's someone you're worried about, then who is he?"

He'd hoped that she wouldn't ask, but he wasn't going to lie to her about that. "He's Lucifer."

Bridget froze before looking up at him. "You mean Lucifer Daystar, the most evil of all fallen angels, has been my guardian throughout the centuries? That doesn't make sense."

Cradling her face in his hands, Mika'il stared down at her. "I know, honey, but he must have done it because he cared for us. He wanted us to be able to find each other again after we were parted too soon all those years ago."

"Does he really care about us that much? I thought Lucifer was a horrible person." Bridget looked confused.

Mika'il snorted. "I know what you mean, but I'm beginning to think he might not be what we thought he was."

"You mean what you thought he was," Bridget pointed out.

"You're right," he muttered before kissing her.

He felt her smile against his lips and happiness flowed through him. He might have been rather judgmental about Lucifer, but it didn't matter.

Nothing mattered except having Bridget in his arms and being able to touch her whenever he wanted.

If he had to thank Lucifer Daystar for that, then he would and he'd do it without being sarcastic or mean. The fallen had given him back the one person he loved in the world. A love he'd never thought he'd be able to see again.

Mika'il had believed there was never going to be a moment in his long life where he held the one he loved while knowing he wasn't going to have to say goodbye to her ever again. He'd thought as an archangel that love and happiness wouldn't be possible. While accepting his lonely existence, he hadn't been able to help wishing that things were different.

"We've spent more centuries than we can count, wishing for things to be different, my brother," Lucifer spoke, his words echoing through Mika'il's head. *"Now things can be, and you can look forward to all those lifetimes to come."*

"Let's grab a cab and go get something to eat. Then maybe go back to your flat for a little afternoon nap. We're going to have a late night," he suggested and she agreed.

* * * *

Later on that night, Mika'il and Bridget entered the Fallen Angel Deux and both cringed slightly at the noise level. A hostess led them to the VIP section where the other Enforcers and their spouses waited.

He shook hands with the men and hugged the ladies before pulling Bridget into the group. "Everyone, this is Bridget Langston."

Teresa gasped. "Oh my God, is this your Bridget?"

He nodded happily and Abby, Danielle, Celeste and Teresa immediately engulfed Bridget. Christian slapped Mika'il on the shoulder.

"Congratulations on finding her again," he said.

"Thank you." Mika'il couldn't help grinning.

"To be honest, I'm surprised you did. How did it happen?" Dominic frowned as he looked at the women.

"It's a long story and one I'll be happy to tell you some other time. Tonight, we're going to celebrate all of us being together and the unexpected gifts of friendship." He thought about Lucifer and how the fallen had given him the most precious gift of all.

"Thank you, Lucifer Daystar."

"You're welcome, Mika'il. I know how much it's cost you to say that to me." Lucifer's voice danced inside his head and for once, there was no arrogance in his tone. *"Love each other and be happy, even only to give me heartburn at how disgustingly joyful you've all become."*

Mika'il glanced around at the people surrounding him. He had never thought he'd call any of them friends again. Yet they were men and women he was proud to consider important in his life.

He put his arm around Bridget, pulling her closer. To have friends and find love were two things that Mika'il had never imagined he'd have. Those two very human experiences weren't supposed to be possible for the head archangel and God's warrior.

A soft warm breeze brushed over his cheek and he smiled, but then a sad thought crossed his mind. *"I wasn't able to find the eighth one, Father."*

"Don't worry, Mika'il. She was never yours to find in the first place. Be happy with what you have now, for I will need you soon."

"Yes, sir."

The other Enforcers met his gaze, having sensed the presence of God, and he shook his head. "It's nothing that needs my attention right now."

"Good because we are here to celebrate. Not only the opening of my new club, but celebrating Mika'il and Bridget finding each other again after all those centuries apart." Dominic raised his glass and the others followed suit. "You are shining examples that true love never dies and that it will wait forever for its chance at happiness."

As the group laughed and talked, Lucifer stood outside the club looking through the windows at them. He wiped a tear from his cross-scarred cheek before turning to walk away. He would give up his soul—if he still had one—to be part of that group again, but circumstances he couldn't change had chased him outside their circle of camaraderie.

Lucifer glared up at the blue sky and considered shaking his fist at God. Yet he knew it wouldn't make him feel any better. He was trapped in this hell of his own choosing, and nothing would free him before it was time.

SAINT PETERSBURG

Dedication

This is for all those people who are misunderstood because they can't explain why they do things. There is no such thing as pure evil or pure good. There are only flawed people doing their best to survive.

Chapter One

Lucifer sat at a table outside the café in Saint Petersburg, Russia, studying the mortals scurrying from building to building. *They're always in such a hurry. Rushing everywhere. Why don't they take the time to appreciate their lives?*

"Because they don't live forever like we do."

He glanced up to see Mika'il standing next to him. Lucifer blinked, but managed not to show any other sign of surprise. He could count on one hand the number of times the archangel had sought him out. Usually he went in search of Mika'il, since irritating him was the only way Lucifer could get the angel to acknowledge him.

"May I sit?" Mika'il gestured to the chair across from Lucifer.

He inclined his head. "Certainly. Would you like some coffee? They have some exquisite blends."

Mika'il pursed his lips while he seemed to contemplate the decision. "Why not? I'm not busy at the moment."

"Really? I thought there was always some mortal you needed to rescue from themselves." He caught the waitress's attention, holding up one finger before pointing at Mika'il. "Plus I would've thought you'd be spending any free time you might have with Bridget — considering you just found each other again."

"Amazingly, Bridget doesn't want to spend all of her time with me. She told me to leave her alone so she could do some painting." Mika'il chuckled as he leaned back to let the girl set his mug on the table. "Why are you here?"

Crossing his legs, Lucifer met Mika'il's questioning gaze. "Am I awake or imagining this? You're asking me why I'm here. Shouldn't I be asking you that? I've never known you to come looking for me."

He watched as Mika'il tasted his coffee and smiled when Mika'il's eyebrows shot up in surprise.

"This is really rather good." Mika'il took another sip before relaxing as he reclined in his seat. "Someone mentioned they had seen you hanging around Saint Petersburg for several months, and I got curious about why you would stay for so long. As far as I know, you don't stay anywhere for more than a minute. If I didn't know better, I'd say you have ADHD."

Lucifer rolled his eyes. "I don't have ADHD, my dear archangel. There is simply nothing in any city in the world that I haven't seen or done already. There's no reason to stay once I complete my mission."

"Then why here? What is here that makes you stay?" Mika'il waved his hand in a vague gesture to include the city around them. "Don't get me wrong. It's a gorgeous city, but I don't think it's any more special than London or Berlin."

Reaching up to touch his cheek, Lucifer looked up at the bright blue sky, though he wasn't seeing it. He was running through the centuries he'd called Saint Petersburg his home, and all the events he'd been a part of or had seen while standing in the shadows. "I've been here almost from the beginning of the city when it was just a fortress to protect the maritime interests of Peter the Great. This is the place I've watched grow over the centuries, and I call it home. I don't like leaving it even for a moment to go somewhere in the world to deal with a problem."

Mika'il frowned and Lucifer could almost see the wheels spinning in the angel's head. "I didn't know you called this home."

"Where did you think I lived?" Lucifer snorted. "Or did you think I didn't sleep or rest at all and just wandered the earth, looking for mortals to trick and souls to steal? Sorry to disappoint you. I'm not as dedicated to my job as you are."

"Shut up. I'm not commenting on your discipline for whatever you're doing on earth. I think you're far more dedicated than you should be. There are times when I would've loved for you to just hole up somewhere to keep the world from going to shit."

Lucifer picked up his cup to take a drink and swallowed before he said, "You do realize that some of those major events I had nothing to do with? I think you're giving me far more credit than I deserve. I'm not as involved in the world as you seem to believe."

The expression on Mika'il's face told Lucifer his former friend didn't believe him, but he didn't care. Not anymore. He'd decided when he'd first returned to Saint Petersburg that he wasn't going to waste his time on trying to get Mika'il to accept him as a friend again. Lucifer had reached a point when he realized it no longer mattered what anyone thought of him. He knew the truth of the situation and that was the only important thing.

"You didn't have anything to do with the Bolshevik Revolution here in 1917?" Mika'il eyed him. "You didn't whisper words of encouragement into those unhappy people's ears to convince them that killing the tsar and his family would make their lives better?"

Lucifer winced. It wasn't because Mika'il had accused him of inciting a coup, but because he had been in Saint Petersburg when the civil war had broken out. He'd watched as madness had swept the city and people had died for no reason other than who they'd been.

Everyone had always believed he enjoyed it when mortals were hurt or killed. Lucifer never could figure out why anyone would think that. Watching anyone suffer used to break his heart, until he'd hardened it so he could stay relatively sane. He didn't want to become like the unrepentants who went into the abyss when God threw them out of Heaven.

It had ceased bothering him that people thought he was in charge of those crazies. He stayed out of their way and they avoided him like he had the bubonic plague. Yet when he heard Mika'il say things like that, Lucifer's heart dropped because he was beginning to think there was never going to be a time when Mika'il treated him as a friend again.

"I had nothing to do with the revolution," Lucifer said, clenching one hand in his lap while picking up his cup with the other. "That came about from the discontent people were feeling. The tsar and his nobles treated them like serfs, and many of the lower classes were as poor as slaves. It was inevitable that they would come to resent the opulence of those who ruled."

Mika'il snorted. "There are ways they could've changed the *status quo* without starting a war to do it."

"Do you really think the tsar would've given up his power if the Bolsheviks had asked him nicely?" Lucifer shook his head. "Nothing earth shattering has ever been done quietly. Changes come in the midst of flame and blood. We have seen it a million times throughout our lifetimes, Mika'il, and we also know that we can't stop it from happening."

"Maybe not, but it wouldn't happen so often if there wasn't unrepentants around, pushing for the hate and anger to explode," Mika'il pointed out. "I don't want to argue with you about this because we both know we're not going to change our minds."

He was more than happy to talk about something else, though he wasn't sure how that was going to happen. Whenever they were together, Mika'il would steer the conversation back to everything going wrong in the world being Lucifer's fault.

"What were you doing here when the revolution broke out?" Mika'il gestured for another cup of coffee.

"Wait. If you want to see, why don't we take a walk through the city?" Pushing to his feet, Lucifer smiled at Mika'il. "It'll be like very old times when we wandered around Heaven, talking about the day."

Mika'il tapped his fingers on the table while staring at him for a moment before he nodded. While he stood, Lucifer pulled out his wallet then threw more than enough *rubles* down to pay for the coffee and leave a nice size tip for the waitress.

Lucifer led the way down the pavement toward the Hermitage, and Mika'il kept pace with him, but didn't say anything. Sticking his hands in the pockets of his slacks, Lucifer stared ahead, following the path without really seeing it. He was remembering the last time he'd dashed down the street, dragging Vera behind him as they ran away from the revolutionaries, plus the other people who were trying to get out of the city as well.

"Are you going to tell me what you were doing, or are we just going to wander Saint Petersburg like tourists?" Mika'il broke down and asked.

Lucifer ducked his head to hide his smirk. He hadn't done it on purpose, but he had known Mika'il wouldn't be able to wait forever for Lucifer to say something. While the archangel had a great deal of patience for the mortals around him, Mika'il didn't always have enough for the angels and fallen he had to deal with all the time, and Lucifer had often felt the brunt of his frustration.

"I was remembering the night of the revolution when the Bolsheviks stormed the Winter Palace. They started the ball rolling here then it swept through the entire country." Lucifer gestured toward the museum. "I'd heard whispers about the communists becoming more and more unhappy. There were rumors that they were planning something, but to my shame, I didn't believe it would truly happen. I was as caught off guard as everyone else when Lenin took over the palace."

"Why didn't you leave?" Mika'il touched his arm, pulling him to a stop.

Lucifer shrugged. "The rumors didn't scare me. Hell, I'm Lucifer. It's not like there's anything people can do to me. I didn't want to leave this city. It had become my home and I wasn't affected by any of the social issues going on in Russia. I wasn't poor or homeless. I was probably richer than even the tsar and his family, but I never threw my money around."

"But the October Revolution was the second one that had happened in Saint Petersburg that year. Why didn't you think the whispers you heard were true?" Mika'il seemed puzzled.

"I thought the communists would be willing to work with the provisional government. Once they got rid of the tsar's rule, I figured they'd be happy." Lucifer curled his lip in annoyance. "I wasn't paying attention to what was going on in my city. I had my mind on other things, like the war being fought throughout Europe. Mortals were dying in mass numbers and I wanted to keep track of what was going on there. I didn't keep an eye on the people in this city."

Mika'il shook his head. "Maybe you should have. Do you think that you might have been able to stop what was going on? If you weren't encouraging them to overthrow the government, why didn't you consider talking them into not doing it?"

Snorting, Lucifer began walking again. "I've watched kingdoms come and go. I've seen emperors and tsars rise and fall. What is one more government's demise when I've seen thousands of them end?"

"See, that's why I get so frustrated. You don't care anymore, Lucifer. At one time you used to worry about all of the mortals on earth. You loved them as much as you loved God."

"Then I got thrown out of Heaven and learned that mortals truly were more beloved of God than his angels." Lucifer held up his hand to keep Mika'il from saying anything else. "Let's not argue about this again, Mika'il."

"Remember all those discussions we had before you left," Mika'il murmured as they continued on their way. "We argued about everything and never agreed on anything. Why is it different now?"

Lucifer fought the urge to smack Mika'il upside the head. "Because now you don't listen to anything I say. You're so sure you know the whole truth, but there is so much you don't know."

The sound Mika'il made was filled with disbelief.

"What about those angels you were supposed to find? The ones God had lost track of somehow, which is really strange because he's God and knows everything, right? So he shouldn't be losing angels like a mortal might lose his pocket watch." Lucifer shook his head.

"How do you know about that? I wanted to ask you in London, but you left before I could pin you down." Mika'il glared at him.

Lifting one shoulder, Lucifer said, "I told you he talks to me sometimes, plus I stalked you to see what you were doing. I noticed something special about the mortals you were doing your level best to hook up with those Enforcers. They weren't the same as the usual suspects. I kept an eye on Bridget and Joan because of that lingering nagging thought that they might be more than they seemed."

"And Cassandra? Why did you visit her throughout the centuries?"

"I needed a friend, and she never entirely blamed me for her fall. Cassandra was always honest that she'd followed me because she wanted the same thing—to be first in God's heart. She never bitched at me about how her life turned out. I appreciated finding someone to talk to without judgment." He paused, not wanting to go into it any further. None of it mattered in the grand scheme of the universe, because Mika'il wasn't inclined to be open-minded about his actions.

"You said saving her and Nevan had nothing to do with her being your friend. You told me it was because the man you killed reneged on a deal he'd made with you."

They reached Palace Square where the Winter Palace stood as part of the State Hermitage—a collection of six buildings housing some of the world's greatest art. Lucifer stopped for a moment, staring at the most beautiful architecture on earth, in his opinion.

"Such works of art," he muttered.

Mika'il hummed softly. "I prefer the Louvre."

"Of course you do." Lucifer gestured toward the entrance of the Winter Palace. "It's Thursday, so the museum is free to visitors today. Let's wander through the rooms while I tell you my story."

He tried not to think of what it had been like to walk into the palace when the tsar had still ruled and the Romanovs had called Saint Petersburg home. He'd attended so many balls and elaborate dinners there. It was where he'd met Vera and had discovered that the devil could lose his heart.

Chapter Two

Petrograd (Saint Petersburg), Russia
June 1914

"Lord Luka Kolwochak," the major-domo announced from the top of the stairs as Lucifer started down into the ballroom.

No one acknowledged his arrival, but he wasn't concerned. Between the noise from the musicians and the conversation, he was surprised anyone could hear anything. He nodded to one of the many nobles who took advantage of the tsar's largesse, though it was more like Tsar Nicholas didn't really care who ate his food or drank his wine.

Nicholas probably didn't even know a majority of the people at the ball, though Lucifer knew each of them and all their secretive thoughts. Nothing was hidden from him.

As he wound his way through the crowd, he smiled but didn't stop to talk with anyone who tried to get him to do so. He wasn't interested in gossiping about which countess was wearing last year's styles, or how much a certain grand duke had lost at the gaming tables the night before.

He spotted General Sukhomlinov standing in an alcove taking to a minister. Lucifer needed to talk to him to find out what was going on with the war. He'd heard rumors that Russia was going to enter the war in support of the Serbs, and he wanted to know if that was the truth.

"General," he said as he approached the duo. Lucifer nodded in the direction of the other minister, noting it was the minister of some domestic bureau which didn't interest him at all.

"Ah, Lord Kolwochak. Glad you could join us tonight." Sukhomlinov shook Lucifer's hand. "I wasn't sure you'd be able to pull yourself away from your work."

"When rumors of war drift by my ears on the summer breeze, I can always find my way free to discover whether they are true or not." Lucifer used a little bit of his power to convince the general that Lucifer could be trusted with state secrets.

Sukhomlinov grimaced before gesturing for Lucifer to follow him. "Excuse us, Minister Barnkov."

The minister bowed then disappeared into the swirling crowd. Sukhomlinov led the way out of the ballroom down one of the many ornately decorated halls to a study. He flagged down a footman and ordered a bottle of champagne be brought to them.

Once they were inside the room, Sukhomlinov waved Lucifer to one of the chairs. Lucifer sat while the general paced. Knowing when it was best to stay silent, Lucifer settled into his seat then watched Sukhomlinov. Finally the general sighed as he turned to look at Lucifer.

"Those whispers of war are true. We're mobilizing troops now and will be marching for the front by August."

Lucifer wanted to protest. More mortals would die, yet he understood why it had to happen. Treaties had to be honored and ancestral ties needed to be recognized. It didn't make him happy though.

"What does Nicholas say about the whole thing?"

Sukhomlinov snorted. "What do you think the tsar says? He wants to lead the army into battle. Like we would let the ruler of our empire go into battle where he could get killed. Foolish man."

"Who will be in charge then?" Lucifer had a few ideas of who they would choose, but the Russians constantly surprised him and didn't always choose who he thought would be the best leader.

"Grand Duke Nikolaevich will be going with the troops to the front."

It wasn't a shock that Nicholas would have appointed his cousin to be commander-in-chief. Lucifer leaned back as a soft knock came from the door and the general ordered whoever it was to come in.

A footman carried a tray in then set it down in front of Lucifer. He poured drinks for them both then left. Lucifer swirled the champagne in his glass, staring into the clear liquid as he processed the information.

"When do you think you'll be making the first advance?" Lucifer glanced up to find Sukhomlinov staring at him. "Yes, sir?"

"Why do you care? You are a very rich man, Lord Kolwochak, and you're not going to fight in any of the regiments. Are you concerned about your serfs and land?" Sukhomlinov slugged back his drink then poured another before wandering away from Lucifer.

"I promise you, Russia will not lose and we will not be invaded by those Germans. We are invincible."

Lucifer fought the urge to roll his eyes. There was no such thing as invincible, especially when mortals were involved. The creatures God loved the most were fragile and they could lose their lives in the simplest of ways.

He shook his head. "I have many financial interests throughout the world, General. This war is starting to interrupt the flow of money into my accounts. I'm trying to figure out if I should leave Petrograd. Maybe go to my property in the country. I have no doubt that you and the army will keep the Germans from invading the Empire."

Lying was easy. So he pretended to be worried about his money and his life, even though neither one would be affected by the war. Lucifer simply wanted to know what was happening around him.

Snorting, Sukhomlinov obviously didn't believe him, but he wasn't interested in that. The general pulled his watch out of his pocket and checked the time. "I need to go back out before the tsar notices I'm missing. He wouldn't be happy if I'm not there to worship at his feet."

After setting his drink down, Lucifer stood to hold his hand out to the general. "Thank you for taking the time to talk to me, General. Our country is lucky to have you watching out for us."

General Sukhomlinov shook his hand then left. Lucifer returned to his chair where he sat, staring into the fireplace filled with summer flowers. This war had the weight of centuries behind it and there was nothing anyone could do to stop it. Hell, he was pretty sure not even God himself would be able to talk sense into either side.

He wondered what Mika'il thought about the whole situation, knowing it was crazy to wish he could talk to the archangel, but he hadn't quite gotten over the fact that he would never return to Heaven to spend time with Mika'il.

Lucifer remembered all those moments when he and Mika'il would walk through Heaven, arguing, yet their discussions had never come between their friendship. No, he'd managed to do to that with his own actions. Sighing, he touched the brand on his left cheek. It still burned from time to time, as did the scars on his back where his wings had been cut from his body.

The sound of the door opening brought him back to the present and Lucifer glanced over to watch a young woman slip into the room. She shut the door then leaned against it with a sigh as she stripped off her gloves. He debated revealing his presence, not wanting to scare her, but no noble young lady should be alone with a strange man. Hell, she shouldn't even be alone with a man she knew if she wasn't related to.

Studying her, he noticed her light brown hair caught in curls at her nape. Her face was narrow with high cheekbones and a slender nose. He couldn't tell what color her eyes were since she had closed them. The dress she wore was white satin with lace on the neckline and the sleeves. Her jewels glimmered in the electric light—diamonds and sapphires around her neck, dripping from her ears and woven through her hair.

He cleared his throat and her eyes popped open. They were hazel. She gasped while pressing her hand to her chest. After standing, he bowed slightly to her.

"I'm sorry to startle you, ma'am. I'm Lord Luka Kolwochak."

She glanced around the room as though she was making sure they really were alone before she said anything. "I'm Lady Vera Turnick, my lord." She started to curtsey, but he gestured for her to stop.

"Come and sit. You look like you were hiding from someone. Trust me when I say they will not find you here." He motioned to the chair across from his.

Vera hesitated for a moment, and he tried to put on his most innocent face, though he knew it was hard to do. His scar and dark eyes tended to be off-putting for some people, and a sweet young girl like Vera wouldn't risk her reputation by being caught in his presence.

Lucifer waited for her to flee the room, but was pleasantly surprised when she approached, then sat. She settled the full skirts of her dress around her then folded her hands in her lap.

"I was hiding, and I thank you for not making a fuss about that."

After taking his own seat, he rested his elbows on the arms of the chair and smiled. "Why would I make a commotion when it gives me a chance to spend time with a very beautiful young woman?"

Rolling her eyes, Vera huffed. "Now you're acting just like the rest of them. I'm not interested in a husband, my lord. I only wish to dance and spend some time with my cousins."

Lucifer held up his hands as though to block himself from her attack. "I'm not looking for a wife either, my lady. Not even one as lovely as you. I have no interest in marriage and no need of money. If you wish to spend time with your cousins, then why are you hiding away in here?"

"Because the male attendees of this ball are having a very difficult time understanding the word 'no'. You would think I was speaking a foreign language the way they stare at me aghast when I tell them I do not wish to walk in the gardens with them." Vera huffed in annoyance, her outrage very obvious.

Hiding his smile by rubbing his jaw, Lucifer commented, "Is this your first time at court?"

"Yes. Father always traveled and Mother hated being away from him, so the entire family would go with him wherever his adventures led." Her jade green eyes seemed to sparkle with happy memories.

"That would explain a lot."

She shot him a questioning glance. Not inclined to answer right away, he poured himself another glass then rested back against the cushions.

"What could that possibly explain?" Vera glared at him.

"My dear girl, you are a beautiful fresh face in the sea of sameness that is swirling around the ballroom right now. All of those boys—and men—don't know what to do with you. Plus, if your family traveled around the world, I'm going to make the assumption that you are rather well-off." He knew proper etiquette said that he shouldn't talk about money around Vera either, but Lucifer never claimed to follow the rules of polite society.

Raising her dark eyebrows in a rather aristocratic glare, Vera said, "It's not polite to discuss things such as this."

"It's not proper for a young, unmarried woman to be alone in the company of a male who is not related to her either," Lucifer pointed out.

She pursed her plump lips while she thought, and Lucifer did his best not to stare at her. He'd had his share of mortal women throughout the millennia he'd lived on earth. It had never been difficult to get them to share his bed. There was something about Vera that seemed just a little different from any of the other ladies Lucifer had met. She didn't look at him like he was a bright shining bauble they'd like to collect, or a rich man who could support them in the life they were accustomed to living.

No, there was something pure in her eyes and the expression on her face. While he thought she was probably innocent about some things, there was a hint of weariness deep beneath the surface of her gaze.

"I will concede that point to you, my lord." Vera nodded her head regally. "But I'm no simpering girl of eighteen, flaunting society and her mother's wrath by hiding away with a strange man. I'm twenty-eight. Quite a spinster, if you were to listen to my mother."

He chuckled this time. "Ah yes. Mothers can be the bane of our existence at times, can they not?"

He could let Vera believe he'd had a mother and a father at one time, though he always made sure to let people know they were dead. That way he didn't have to produce them to meet anyone.

"Yes. At least mine can be. Now that war has broken out in Europe, she's decided it would be a good time for us to come home. Visit family and see the home none of us has ever lived in." Vera fidgeted with one of the ruffles on her skirt. "When Aunt Svetlana, the Countess Palen, offered to have me come visit her, I must admit Mother was so thrilled."

"And you were not?" The knowledge that Vera must be related to the royal family wasn't important. In the end, it didn't matter to him whether she was in direct line for the throne or not. Blood, money and social standing had no effect on him at all.

She peered up at him for a moment as though she were gauging his reaction to her revelation. When she seemed satisfied, she answered his question. "It has always been my dream to come and visit my aunt and Petrograd. I also hoped to meet the royal family. While we are very distantly related to them, I have never had the privilege of meeting them. When Aunt Svetlana asked for me to come stay, I quickly agreed."

Lucifer nodded. "It was nice of the countess to open her home to you. I'm sure your cousins are happy to have you here as well. Have you spent much time with the royal family? They are quite reclusive. I was surprised when the ball was announced, actually. It has been a while since one was held here."

"They have given me a very warm welcome so far," Vera informed him.

"Won't your aunt come looking for you?" Lucifer waved his hand at the door. "I'm sure someone must be wondering where you went."

Vera shook her head. "I told her I was going to one of the retiring rooms, but I haven't learnt how to travel along all the hallways and corridors. I became lost then I spotted one of my ardent suitors. I had to hide before he saw me."

"Which is why you are here, sitting in a drawing room while chatting with a stranger." Lucifer grinned. "Your suitor has probably returned to the ballroom or one of the gaming rooms. I think you could safely sneak out and ask a footman to take you to the right place."

"Are you trying to get rid of me, Lord Kolwochak?" There was a hint of a smile at the edges of her lips.

"Certainly not, Lady Vera. That would be ungentlemanly of me. I'm happy to share my quiet space with you for as long as you'd like." He looked at the bottle of liquor. "I hesitate to ask, but find I must. Would you like a drink?"

Wrinkling her nose, Vera said, "No thank you. I much prefer champagne to any of our native drinks."

After taking a sip, Lucifer nodded. "I must admit, I agree with you, but it wasn't I who ordered the refreshments in the first place."

Silence filled the area between them for a few minutes while Lucifer's mind went back to the coming war. He worried about it, since there were unrepentants and Enforcers fighting on both sides. Would the unrepentants take advantage of the chaos and cause more death and destruction?

Lucifer had seen hundreds of wars over the course of the millennia he'd been forced to endure on earth. He'd watched mortals kill each other over foolish things and inconsequential land. Maybe because he was Lucifer Daystar, the most evil of all fallen, he should revel in the blood and pain war brought, but he'd never been able to find happiness in death.

Chapter Three

Petrograd, Russia
June 1914

Vera found herself studying the silent man sitting across from her. His blond hair glittered gold in the lamplight and his expression was rather sad as he stared down at the liquor in his glass. She'd noticed him when he'd strolled through the ballroom earlier. How could she not have?

Tall and blond like a Nordic god, he'd stood out among the shorter, darker Russians and had caught her eye. Vera had had a few suitors while her family traveled the world, but none of them had created such a visceral reaction as this man did at her first look at him.

She'd asked Cousin Maria, Aunt Svetlana's oldest daughter, who he was and she had eyed Vera knowingly before telling her his name. It was a little embarrassing when a rather innocent nineteen-year-old could tell how interested in the man she was.

Lord Kolwochak had caught her attention and Vera wanted to know more about him, but she hadn't planned on ending up sitting in a room alone with him. Maria had given her some whispered gossip about Kolwochak, letting Vera know he was considered a man an innocent woman like her shouldn't even be thinking about.

A clearing throat caused her to blink and she saw Kolwochak looking back at her. She was a little embarrassed to be caught staring.

"How did you get that scar?" She gestured toward the cross-shaped brand on his left cheek.

He touched it with a brief brush of his fingers. "It's a reminder of foolish choices."

As much as she wanted to ask, she didn't have any right to do that. They'd just met and it wasn't her place to dig into all of his secrets. Also, she didn't want him digging through hers, because there were some things in her past that she didn't want brought to light.

"It does give you a rather dashing look. I'm sure the girls throw themselves at you." She laughed. "You must be causing quite a stir, like a wolf amongst the sheep."

His gaze on her felt like he was touching her and she shivered, not happy with the urge she had to run her fingers over his skin. Vera clenched her hands to keep from reaching out.

"I don't know about that," he said and smiled slightly. "I haven't paid much attention to what is going on at the balls and soirees."

"Are you watching what is going on in Europe? I'm sure you—like a lot of the nobles—have money interests that will be affected by this war, Lord Kolwochak." Vera tried not to think about all of her friends who had become displaced or endangered by the fighting.

"Hmm…that is one of the reasons why I asked about their plans. Please, call me Luka when we're alone."

His voice caused her to press her thighs together. It brushed over her like the softest fur. After she swallowed, she nodded. "Then you must call me Vera. Not that we'll be spending any more time alone, Luka. I do believe it is time I return. Maria, my cousin, and the others will be wondering what has happened to me."

Vera stood and Luka pushed to his feet as well. She inhaled sharply when he took a step into her personal space. There was the oddest fragrance of cinnamon and sulfur, and she didn't know if it came from him or from elsewhere in the room.

"I'll be happy to escort you until we reach the doorway of the ballroom. It would do nothing for your reputation to be seen returning with me." Luka offered his elbow. "I promise not to take any liberties."

"What if I want you to?" she blurted then bit her tongue in embarrassment.

Luka's eyebrows shot up while he stared at her then a sly smile lifted the corners of his lips. He encircled her waist before easing her closer. Resting her hands on his chest, she looked up at him.

Vera wasn't a virgin, no matter what her parents thought, but the butterflies in her stomach seemed to be warning her that kissing Luka would change her world in a fundamental way. She shivered when he cupped the back of her head in his hand.

"Are you sure about this, Vera?" he asked, pausing long enough for her to change her mind if she wanted.

No, she wasn't sure about it at all, but she wanted his mouth on hers, if only for this one instance in time. She nodded and he lowered his head.

The moment their lips touched, the world disappeared around her. Vera forgot about the hundreds of people filling the palace and the possibility they might be discovered. She didn't care if the building crumbled to the ground.

Luka held her tight and her breasts tingled as they were crushed against his solid chest. Moaning low in her throat, Vera slid her arms around his neck and opened to his demands. When Luka swept his tongue in, she tasted the liquor he'd had earlier. She didn't protest as he placed one of his hands on her butt. The silk of her dress absorbed the heat coming from his body, and warmth pooled at the junction of her thighs.

"Oh my," she whispered as he left her mouth to trail kisses along her jaw then down her neck.

He nipped at her collarbone before pressing his tongue to the fluttering pulse at the base of her throat. Vera couldn't catch her breath enough to ask what he was doing when he lifted her. She just tightened her hold on him then gasped as he sat on the settee in the corner farthest from the door.

"What are you doing?" she managed to ask.

"I'm kissing you again," Luka informed her before he swooped down to press his lips to hers fiercely.

Again all coherent thought rushed from her mind and Vera found herself in a sea of sensation. She whimpered when he palmed her breast, rubbing his fingers over her hard nipple. Arching, she tried to beg for more with her silent movements, but Luka seemed to proceed at his own pace.

He gentled their embrace, easing her nerves before she even realized she was nervous. Vera had never thought she was wanton or loose. Of course, she hadn't been the type of woman who believed she needed to save herself for marriage either. Her family might be related to the tsar, but they weren't important enough for her to be called upon to make a political marriage.

Luka nibbled along the tops of her breasts and Vera slid her fingers through his blond hair to hold his mouth to the swells of her chest. His tongue slipped in the valley of her mounds then he blew a puff of air over the wet area, causing her to shiver.

She jumped when his hand touched her knee underneath her dress. Tension drew her muscles tight and she stiffened in his arms. He pulled back, removing his mouth and his hand from her skin. Vera fought the urge to protest, to beg him to keep touching her. It wasn't proper to do this with a man she'd just met a few minutes ago.

While she might be a worldly woman, she was unmarried, and being found in such a compromising situation could force her to marry a man she knew nothing about. Licking her lips, she began to slow her breathing.

"I'm sorry, Lady Vera." Luka settled her next to him, putting a little bit of space between them. "I seem to have lost control and taken advantage of your pleasant nature."

She couldn't help snorting. "My family would be happy to tell you that I don't have a pleasant nature, my lord. You didn't take anything that I wasn't willing to give you, but I do believe it is best that I return to my aunt."

After standing, he offered her his hand then assisted her to her feet. "I'll let you go on your own, Vera. I fear if I spend more time in your company while alone, I will fall back into my disgraceful behavior, which you might not wish to experience again."

Vera strolled to the door then turned to flash a smile in Luka's direction. "I think you should come and be introduced, my lord. Then maybe we should dance and learn about each other."

Luka frowned and a strangely sad expression crossed his face quickly before a practiced smile appeared. "I'm not sure you will wish to continue our acquaintance once you learn more about me, my lady, but I will honor your request."

She dipped her head regally then opened the door a few inches, wanting to check the hallway before she left.

"There's no one out there," Luka told her and she glanced at him. He shrugged off her silent question. "I have very good hearing and I haven't heard any footsteps for the last few minutes. The corridor is deserted, so you're safe to leave."

Is that really true? She peeked up then down the hallway. It was empty so she stepped out, not looking back. While she might have just met Luka, she believed he would do as he said and come to be formally introduced to her.

Vera tugged on her gloves while stopping in front of a mirror just outside the ballroom. She checked to make sure her hair and dress looked all right and didn't show any sign of what had happened in the room she'd just been in. Everything looked perfect except for her flushed cheeks and swollen lips. Taking a deep breath, she did her best to slow her pulse and breathing.

Once she figured she was calm, she walked into the ballroom, sweeping her gaze over the sea of people to see if she could spot her aunt or one of her cousins who were old enough to attend the evening's entertainment.

"There you are, Vera. I was just about to come looking for you." Maria emerged from the crowd, not paying attention to those who bowed or curtsied as she went past. She laid her hand on Vera's arm. "You are feeling all right, Cousin?"

"Yes, dear. I'm fine. I ended up getting lost in the wonderful halls. Finally, I found a footman to direct me back here." Vera chuckled. "It will take me some time to learn all the ins and outs of this place."

Maria smiled as she took Vera's hand then started to lead her over to where the other ladies sat with Aunt Svetlana. "I'm not sure it's possible to memorize the corridors and rooms of the Winter Palace, Vera. It is like the emperors chose to make it as confusing as possible."

"It is truly one of the wonders of the world and the Amber Room is simply marvelous," Vera gushed, not lying about what she thought of the palace.

"I have always loved that room," Maria admitted as they sat. "It is stunning and will — I'm sure — stand as a monument of Russian superiority."

Vera covered her unladylike snort with a cough. Russian superiority? While she was proud of her homeland, she didn't see them as any better than any other country. "You are probably right about that, Maria."

A throat being cleared brought their attention to where Luka stood in front of them. He smiled at Aunt Svetlana.

"My lady, it is wonderful to see you again. Forgive me for not coming to greet you sooner. I had some business to take care of before I could begin the rest of my night." Luka took Vera's aunt's hand in his then bowed over it.

"My Lord Kolwochak, it is always a pleasure to see you." Svetlana's smile held a hint of flirtation.

"And who are these beautiful young women sitting with you? I didn't know you had any sisters." He nodded toward Vera and her cousins.

Svetlana giggled at Luka's compliment and Vera wanted to comment on the foolish way her aunt was acting toward Luka. While he might have been pretending to flirt with Svetlana, Vera could tell all of his attention was on her.

"These are my daughters. Maria, Oksana and Ana. Also, my niece is joining us for the summer. Lady Vera Turnick. Everyone, this is Lord Luka Kolwochak. He is a good friend of your father's." Svetlana waved her hand in the direction of a chair close to them. "Would you care to sit, my lord?"

Luka shook his head. "I think I would like to dance, ma'am. Do I have your permission to do so with your niece?"

Svetlana looked surprised that Luka was asking to dance with Vera, but she didn't say anything as she nodded. Luka offered his hand to Vera who took it with as much nonchalance as she could. Showing any kind of excitement wouldn't endear her to her cousins or aunt. She got the feeling Luka was seen as a great prize amongst the ladies of the Russian nobility.

Happiness colored her smile when he led her out onto the floor just as the band struck up a waltz. They wouldn't be able to dance as closely as she would've liked, but at least he'd hold her in his arms.

"I think you've caused quite a stir with my cousins," she commented as they whirled around the floor in perfect rhythm with each other.

"Why do you say that?" Luka didn't take his gaze off her up-turned face.

"Just from their expressions. Also, I'm sure they are all scheming out plans on how to be the next one you dance with." She laughed. "You might end up quite tired before you are done dancing."

Luka shook his head. "I'll only be dancing with you, Vera. I have no interest in young, silly girls who think of marriage and love."

She raised her eyebrow. "Are you saying I'm old and not looking for those same things?"

"You aren't old, but you are mature enough to know that there is no such thing as instant love. That first flash of attraction — or lust — can be mistaken for love." Luka swung her around then settled back into the waltz's grand dance. "Those emotions can grow into stronger ones after a couple is given time to learn about each other. You understand that."

"What? That love takes time to grow?" At his nod, she pursed her lips and thought about it for a moment. "I guess you are right, my lord. I have experienced both the instant lust and the enduring love. Or at least what I thought was enduring love. To my surprise, his love only lasted long enough for him to take my innocence, then he left to find a virgin bride who was richer than me."

Luka's dark eyes flashed red for a second and Vera blinked, wondering how her own eyes could play tricks on her like that.

"You were seduced?"

Shrugging, she said, "Yes, but you see, I wanted to be. I was a willing participant in my deflowering, Luka. Don't think I didn't know what I was doing. Yes, I thought I loved him. Yet it doesn't matter in the end because he didn't love me. It is a common occurrence amongst naves and rakes."

"You don't sound very upset about it?" He stroked his thumb over her hand and it was as though he touched her naked skin.

Shivering, she replied, "No. I'm not upset about it. I cried when he jilted me, which is only right since no woman wants to find out the man she loved wasn't a gentleman."

He inclined his head. "You are right about that, though I wouldn't know from personal experience."

"You've never been seduced then left with your heart bleeding?" she teased.

The overwhelming sadness in his eyes almost brought her to tears then it disappeared behind his façade of calm indifference. "Once when I was young and foolish, I believed someone loved me enough to never turn their back on me. The lesson I learned from their betrayal was harsh and swift."

Her heart ached for the pain his words hinted at. None of the men who had hurt her had broken her soul like Luka's seemed to be. She wanted to wrap her arms around him and hold his head pressed to her chest. Vera wished she could whisper that she would never do that to him.

She laughed silently at herself. Luka wouldn't want some woman to treat him like a frightened child. He was a grown man who must have forged his own way in what could be a hostile world. Something in the tilt of his head and the brace of his shoulders told her he'd fought for every inch of ground and every *ruble* he'd gained. Nothing had ever been given to him.

"I'm sorry" was all she could think of to say.

He touched her cheek with gentle fingers. "Thank you, my lady, but it was not your fault that I was naïve and eager to please. I discovered a strength I never realized I had from that experience."

"And you don't trust as easily as you once did," she announced, having read between the lines of what he'd said.

Bowing his head in acknowledgment, Luka smiled. "You're right, my dear Vera. Trust once broken is very difficult to repair and it can take centuries to even establish a common place to rebuild it."

"Centuries? No one has that kind of time." She giggled then sighed as the music ended. "I guess our dance has ended, my lord."

"This one perhaps, but never doubt that I will come dance with you again before the night is over." He stepped back then lifted her hand to his lips.

She longed for him to press his mouth to her bare skin instead of the gloves she wore, but they were in a room full of people who would gossip and tear her reputations to shreds. While she might not care overly much about her own, she didn't want anything she did to reflect badly on her aunt.

Luka returned her to Aunt Svetlana and bowed once again before disappearing into the crowd. Vera found herself surrounded by her cousins and several other young ladies. Who knew one dance with a handsome man would make her the most popular person at the ball?

She savored the feeling while looking forward to their next dance. Even though she'd just met him, she believed him when he'd said he would be back for another one before the night was over.

Chapter Four

Saint Petersburg
Present day

"You seduced an innocent girl during a ball at the Winter Palace." Mika'il sounded unhappy, but not surprised.

Lucifer studied the chandeliers hanging from the ceiling of the Great Hall where he'd danced with Vera for the first time all those years ago. He didn't look at the archangel as he spoke. "Vera wasn't innocent in many ways, Mika'il. She didn't hesitate to kiss me back. If there had been any doubt whatsoever in her, I wouldn't have done anything more than brush her cheek."

"Still, Lucifer. Then you danced with her. What were you thinking?"

Whirling to glare at Mika'il, he said, "That I wanted to be normal for once in my pathetic, fucked-up life. Maybe for just one moment I wanted to be mortal and hold a beautiful woman in my arms that I didn't have to seduce or glamour into being there. Vera didn't see me as anything more than a man, broken and secretive, but still no different than any other male she'd danced with for most of her life."

Mika'il took a step back from his fury. "But you aren't normal or mortal, and never will be. Isn't that why you rebelled in the first place? Because you wanted God to love us more than he did these fragile creatures?"

Lucifer looked to where Mika'il pointed. There was a group of tourists at the other end of the Great Hall, listening to their guide. Only one of them stared back at him. The little brunette girl smiled at him and waved. He waved back before turning away from her. She could see through their power that kept the adults from spotting them.

"That's right. I'd forgotten why I chose to rise up against God." Sarcasm thickened his voice. "It's not like you have ever allowed that to slip my mind. You bring it out every time we meet. Maybe you should go back and re-examine what really happened."

"Are you saying I missed something? That things didn't happen the way I think they did?" Mika'il folded his arms over his chest while studying Lucifer. "Why should I listen to you?"

Rolling his eyes, Lucifer turned away. "You're right, Mika'il. You shouldn't believe me because I've done nothing to change your mind. I'm still the same arrogant asshole I've always been."

He stalked toward one of the hallways that led to a specific room, not caring if Mika'il followed him or not. He wanted to see the space where he'd met Vera, the only woman he'd ever loved and who had loved him for no other reason than that she'd thought he was a good man.

"Did she know who and what you are? Did you ever tell her the truth?" Mika'il's question drifted along behind him.

"No. I never needed to reveal the truth." After opening the door of the study, he stepped inside and was almost instantly transported back to that night. Then Mika'il joined him, destroying all his happy memories. "Vera and I fell in love because she never wanted anything more from me than my heart. She healed the broken pieces in me then I lost her."

"How could you lose one small mortal female?" Mika'il shook his head as he walked past Lucifer to move deeper into the room.

"How could God lose eight angels?" He grinned at the dismayed expression on the archangel's face. "I know you thought you were the only one who knew about the angels you were looking for. I told you back in London. You aren't the only one God talks to from time to time."

"Why would he talk to you? I don't understand that," Mika'il muttered as he stuffed his hands in his pockets while pacing.

Lucifer didn't feel like discussing that with his former friend. If God hadn't seen fit to fill Mika'il in, then Lucifer wasn't either. It wasn't his place to explain things to Mika'il.

"She snuck in here to hide from an over-eager suitor," Lucifer murmured.

"That's what you said. What happened after you danced with her that night?" Mika'il seemed willing to shelf the discussion of the lost angels for another time.

After wandering over to one of the chairs, he sat then snapped his fingers. A bottle of Zyr vodka appeared on the table in front of him along with two highball glasses. "Would you like a drink?"

The sound coming out of Mika'il had the tone of annoyance to it, but Lucifer didn't care. He wasn't around to entertain the archangel or make him happy by being accommodating. After pouring a glass, he set it down on the edge closest to Mika'il before getting some for himself.

He took a sip then settled back into the cushions. Lucifer crossed his legs and smiled as Mika'il sat in the other chair before he picked up his own drink.

"I danced with Vera again. I made sure to dance with her cousins and aunt as well. I wasn't quite willing to single her out just yet. The noble families were already talking about her because I chose to dance with her twice." He shook his head. "I should've known better, but I couldn't stay away. There was something about her that intrigued me."

"When did you become lovers?"

Smirking, Lucifer met Mika'il's gaze. "I never kiss and tell, Mika'il. You should know that. I wouldn't think you'd be interested in my love life."

"I'm not stupid. I know you wouldn't have spent all that time with Vera without bedding her." Mika'il fidgeted with the glass in his hands. "You're not an innocent virgin, Lucifer."

"That's true. I haven't been since shortly after I was thrown out of heaven. Why try to keep myself pure when I would never be returning home?" He shoved the bitterness that simmered in his heart down, wishing he'd learned how to deal with the pain of his isolation.

After so many millennia, he should've been able to forget about what he'd lost and accept what he had. There were so many things he'd discovered while wandering the earth throughout the centuries, yet nothing had made up for being exiled from the home he loved and the people he'd considered his brothers and sisters. Nothing had until he'd met Vera, then he'd found someone to show him the wonders of the world around him.

Mika'il grimaced then nodded. "I guess you're right about that, and really, I don't want to know anything about your love life. I'm sure you didn't seduce her, though you could've."

"My dear friend, I've seduced more than my fair share of women, but I didn't even try with Vera. In fact, she seduced me," he admitted as he smiled faintly.

"I don't want to hear about it. How the heck did you manage to lose her though? That's what I don't understand." Mika'il finished his liquor then poured another drink.

Lucifer shrugged, not interested in talking about that part. He hated the idea that he'd managed to misplace the one person he really loved.

"The war had gone well the first two weeks for the Russian army. They'd achieved some victories along the Western front and I'm sure they thought they'd be able to roll into Germany without opposition. Then the Germans proved to be a tougher opponent than they had assumed. Massive fatalities were suffered on both sides." He tapped his fingers on his thigh as he thought about the first months of the war effort.

"Overconfidence has always been the bane of military leaders. The Grand Duke should've known better," Mika'il commented.

From what Lucifer knew about the leader of the Russian army, it hadn't necessarily been his fault. "Once he started losing and the tsar showed up, every order seemed to be countermanded by letters from Saint Petersburg. The empress was listening to Rasputin, and Nicholas would do as her letters said."

Mika'il shook his head. "I can't imagine what that particular fallen was doing, trying to control a war like that. What did he hope to gain?"

"I don't know. He wasn't an unrepentant, or at least I couldn't tell he'd gone over to the abyss. Rasputin wasn't interested in causing the death of anyone. I'm still not sure how they managed to kill him, unless there was an Enforcer amongst the assassins." He shot Mika'il a glance.

The archangel lifted one shoulder. "I can't be sure there wasn't. I don't have command over every single one of them. I have a general idea of where they are at any given time, but to say for sure that one of them killed Rasputin, I can't. Did you ever meet him?"

Lucifer nodded. "It was the end of 1914."

Chapter Five

Petrograd, Russia
December 1914

"Luka," Vera whispered into his ear as she leaned on him in the carriage. "Where are we going?"

Lucifer turned to look at her and because she was so close, his lips brushed hers. He cradled the back of her head, doing his best not to mess up her hair as he took their kiss deeper. She opened to him and he swept his tongue in to stroke along hers.

Vera rested her hands on his shoulders, bracing herself against the sway of the vehicle. Lucifer gripped her waist to keep her from falling over while they embraced. One of the wheels hit a bump and she bit his tongue.

Pulling away, he chuckled when she tried to apologize. "It's all right, Vera. My tongue's still attached."

He stroked her cheek as she settled back onto the cushions, but she stayed close to him. They had been spending time with each other since they'd met in

June. He'd escorted her and her cousins to various balls and soirees. They'd been riding in the parks where other members of the nobility could see them together.

Vera was the first mortal he'd ever spent so much time with. Usually, he'd bed the women then move on. After millennia, he'd discovered there was no point to getting attached to any of them. In fact, he'd never met one he wanted to spend more than a night with.

Until Vera had appeared in the study, intriguing him with her bluntness and purity. Oh, not of body but of spirit. He knew she wasn't a virgin, which astonished him since young ladies of titled families were kept sequestered away until they were sold to the highest bidder—money or title wise.

"Are you going to tell me where we are going?" Vera poked him in the side, bringing his attention back to her.

"We're going to the Alexander Palace. Empress Alexandra and the Grand Duchesses have ordered me to bring you to them. They wish to meet you because I have mentioned you to them once or twice."

Her mouth dropped open and she stared at him in shock. After reaching over to shut her mouth, he laughed.

"I can't believe you didn't tell me this beforehand, Luka. I would've worn a nicer dress and done my hair better." She fluttered her hands anxiously.

"My dear, you look lovely as usual. The Empress will think you are enchanting like I do." He took her hand in his. "Just breathe."

She glared at him. "You could have warned me. This isn't like going to meet your family, Luka. This is

Empress Alexandra and her daughters. If they don't like me, they could have me killed."

Coughing to cover up his laughter, Lucifer squeezed her hand. "I won't let them kill you."

"You can't do anything about it. You're just one of her subjects. You have no control over what she does and doesn't do." She shook her head as though she thought he was crazy to believe he could do otherwise.

He bit his tongue, fighting the urge to tell her that there were only two beings in the entire universe that didn't bow down to his authority. She'd never doubted his story of being a man who'd made his fortune then was granted a title by the tsar for services he'd done the empire. Of course, none of it was true, but that didn't matter. No one was going to challenge him.

"I didn't even know you were personal friends with the royal family. They are very private people." Vera tilted her head as she studied him. "Why would they want to see me? Just how close are you to them?"

"The tsar has been busy in meetings for the war, and the empress is a little lonely, so I told her about you and she ordered me to bring you today. Please don't panic too much. She actually is a very nice lady."

Blinking, Vera said, "She's a nice lady? Alexandra Feodorovna, the Empress of All the Russias isn't a nice lady. She's not the slightly dotty grandmother no one talks about at family gatherings. Her husband is one of the most powerful men in the world with millions of soldiers at his command. She could have me jailed for looking at her wrong."

Lucifer snorted, unsure how to deal with her fear. Nothing he said seemed to make her feel safe, yet he was the safest person for her to be with because there was no way anyone could hurt her in his presence.

Before he could say anything, the carriage came to a stop. They listened to footsteps come closer, then the door opened. A footman appeared, holding the door. After climbing out, Lucifer turned to offer his hand to Vera and help her from the vehicle.

He could feel her tremble in his grip, so he lifted her knuckles to his lips before brushing a quick kiss over them. "You are beautiful, Vera, and have as much right to be in the presence of the empress as she does to be in yours. Remember that. It is merely an accident of birth that makes her royal instead of you."

Vera's face brightened at his whispered words and she nodded. With that, he offered her his arm. Once she took it, he turned them so they could walk up the steps to one of the side doors into the Alexander Palace. He knew it led into one of the smaller but still formal greeting chambers.

"Please wait here, my Lord Kolwochak. I'll inform the empress that you and Lady Turnick have arrived." Alexandra's personal secretary told them before she left the room.

He could tell that Vera didn't want to sit, so Lucifer strolled around the room, pointing out the paintings on the wall and discussing them. He'd known a few of the artists while they were creating their masterpieces. He did his best to keep her mind off what was going to happen in a few minutes.

"They are ready to see you now, my lord and lady."

Lucifer patted Vera's hand as he gestured for the secretary to show them where to go. Of course, he'd been there so often, he knew where the empress would be seeing them, but he had to observe the formalities.

"Lord Luka Kolwochak and Lady Vera Turnick, Tsarina," the secretary announced.

Luka bowed low while Vera swept into a deep curtsy. They stayed like that until a soft voice told them to rise. He lifted his eyes to meet the shy gaze of Alexandra.

Tsarina Alexandra Feodorovna, the Empress-Consort of All the Russias, was not a beautiful woman. She was handsome though, and had a regal bearing. If she were walking down a city street, no one would mistake her for anything other than royalty.

"It is wonderful to see you again, Luka. I'm happy you were able to join us today." Alexandra held out her hand and Luka obliged her by kissing the back of it.

"I could never miss out on visiting my favorite ladies," he teased gently.

Olga, Tatiana, Maria and Anastasia circled around him and he made sure to greet each one individually. The grand duchesses were a marvelous group of young women. Lucifer had enjoyed talking to them.

"Please introduce us to your companion," Alexandra commanded politely.

"Empress Alexandra, this is Lady Vera Turnick. Her aunt is Lady Svetlana, Countess Palen." Lucifer brought Vera forward. "Lady Vera, may I introduce you to Tsarina Alexandra and the Grand Duchesses Olga, Tatiana, Maria and Anastasia."

Vera curtsied again, but Alexandra stopped her.

"Lady Vera, come sit next to me and tell me about your parents. I have met your aunt, Countess Palen, but I don't believe I've had the privilege of knowing your family." Alexandra motioned to the chair next to her chaise longue.

Lucifer watched as Vera took her seat. He smiled as he noticed both Vera and the empress try to overcome their shyness to start a conversation, but soon Vera had relaxed enough to keep the discussion going. Olga and Tatiana stayed close to their mother, retrieving items whenever the empress asked for them.

He took a chair a few feet away and soon found himself talking to Anastasia about something she and Alexi, the tsarevich, had done earlier in the day. Maria had wandered off a little way to work on some sort of sewing.

They all chatted for a while when a different kind of air filled the room. Lucifer glanced up to see Rasputin enter. He'd heard all about the mystic healer the tsar had ensconced in the family home to help Alexei. Everyone knew the young heir was sickly and the tsarina fretted over her son.

"Father Grigori, come join us." Alexandra waved her hand at him. "I wish you to meet Lord Luka Kolwochak and Lady Vera Turnick."

The minute Rasputin's gaze met Lucifer's, they recognized each other. Every fallen in the world knew who Lucifer was and they feared him almost more than they feared God. Rasputin paled, but Lucifer wasn't inclined to do anything to the fallen unless Rasputin thwarted his own plans.

"Father, I have heard miraculous things about you." Lucifer shook Rasputin's hand.

Lucifer saw Rasputin shudder as Lucifer's power rolled over him. There was no doubt Grigori Rasputin was a very powerful fallen, yet he was no match for Lucifer.

"Thank you, my lord, but any power I have comes from the Father in Heaven." Rasputin ducked his head in deference to Lucifer's superiority.

"That is true of us all, Father." Alexandra rang a bell. "The servants will be bringing in some tea for us. How is Alyosha this afternoon?"

Rasputin strolled over to where Alexandra lay, touching his fingers to the back of her hand before taking a seat on the other side of her. "Your son is doing very well, Empress. He is resting at the moment. Gilliard is with him, as well as Derevneko."

Vera seemed a little overwhelmed to be in the presence of the royal family and Rasputin. Lucifer understood. It must have been much like meeting legendary people she'd always heard about, but never truly believed existed until she saw them with her own eyes.

The next several hours went by quickly as Lucifer did his best to ensure everyone had a lovely time. While he didn't especially want Vera to be welcomed into the royal family with open arms, he did want her to see that for all intents and purposes, the Romanovs were just like any other family. Sure, they happened to rule a large country, but besides that, they had all the same squabbles and enjoyment as anyone else.

The sun was setting when Lucifer decided they should probably be returning to Petrograd. Alexandra insisted it was too dark out for them to travel the roads and she offered them rooms at the palace. There wasn't any way Lucifer could refuse.

He accepted and Vera wrote a note to her aunt, telling her where she was and that she would be availing herself of the empress's hospitality. Alexandra sent a groomsman off with the letter then had one of the maids show them to their suites. After he'd freshened up, Lucifer went in search of Vera.

Her room was right next to his, and he let a smile skip across his face. As he was about to knock on her door, a footman approached him.

"Lord Kolwochak, the empress wishes to express her regrets, but she and the grand duchesses will be unable to attend dinner with you and Lady Turnick tonight. She suggests that you enjoy a private meal in your suite."

"That will be fine. Please, have everything set up in my sitting room," he ordered and the footman bowed before leaving.

Once he was alone again, he knocked then waited until he heard Vera call for him to come in. He found her standing by the window, staring out into the garden her room overlooked.

"Have you enjoyed yourself today?" he asked, truly wanting to know.

She dashed over to him before throwing her arms around him. "Thank you so much, Luka. It's like a dream." After pressing a quick kiss to his cheek, she whirled away and laughed. "Imagine me having luncheon and tea with the empress and her daughters then spending the night in the palace. Aunt Svetlana and the girls aren't going to believe this."

"You'll be the belle of a hundred balls while everyone tries to get you to gossip about what you saw here," he informed her.

Vera shook her head. "Oh no. I couldn't trade on the empress's generosity."

Huffing softly, Lucifer said, "You wouldn't be the first or the last to do so."

"I know, but just because others do it doesn't mean I should." She returned to the window. "They were very nice, not at all what I thought they would be like."

"In many ways, Alexandra has got a bad reputation and her subjects don't seem willing to give her a chance to win them over, not even now, after so many years." Lucifer shrugged. "I'm not sure the chasm can be repaired."

He'd sensed a dark cloud hanging over the royal family that afternoon while they visited. Seeing the future wasn't one of his gifts, but he had the uneasy feeling things were going to get worse for the Romanovs in the months and years to come. He'd met Rasputin's gaze and seen the same knowledge in the fallen's eyes.

There were times when Lucifer wished he could interfere in the lives of the mortals, but there were limits to what he was allowed to do. While making deals for their souls wasn't frowned upon, saving them from their destinies was.

Sighing, Vera nodded. "You're right. Are we having dinner with them? I'm certainly not dressed for that."

"No. I'm pretty sure visiting with us has worn Alexandra out. She is fragile in so many ways. She and the girls will be dining *en famille* tonight. They're bringing ours to my sitting room, so we can eat there." He took her hand to pull her close to him. Leaning down, he nuzzled her jaw before nibbling on her earlobe. "It would give us a chance to be alone without any chaperones."

Her sharply inhaled breath told him she liked the way his thoughts were leading. "Let's go. I would like to see if your suite looks any different than mine."

He glanced around once before heading toward the door. "Mine is decorated in greens instead of blues, but they are much the same."

Vera nodded, but he could tell she wasn't really listening to him. "Why did my aunt let me come here with you without having to bring one of my maids?"

Lucifer shrugged, not about to tell her that he'd influenced her aunt's mind into giving her permission for them to travel alone together. He was tired of chaperones with their disapproving stares and unhappy sighs. It wasn't like he was going to strip Vera naked in the middle of the opera and take her in his box. He simply wanted to talk to her without anyone listening and to be able to kiss her without worrying about her reputation being tarnished.

"I don't know, but I think having the empress in residence with us will keep you from becoming fodder for the gossips." He squeezed her hand. "Come. I'm sure they'll have set a table and chairs for us by now."

* * * *

Luka had been right. The table and chairs were set in a small alcove that overlooked the same garden Vera could see from her room. There were two footmen to serve them and Vera kept her hands from shaking as much as she could. She knew what would be happening after dinner was finished and the servants left.

Nerves caused her stomach to flutter, so she wasn't able to enjoy the rich food, and her cousins would be very disappointed when they asked her to describe what she ate. She couldn't remember a single thing once the dishes and everything had disappeared.

Vera didn't understand why she felt so anxious about sharing a bed with Luka. It wasn't like she was a virgin, having been deflowered several years ago by an Italian count who'd moved on to the next innocent maid before Vera could work out exactly what had happened. She'd been horrified and heartbroken, but had recovered while realizing that what she'd given the man wasn't that important—at least in her mind, anyway.

Once they were alone in the sitting room, Luka stood then offered her his hand. She knew what he was silently asking, and she held his gaze as she placed hers in his. This was something she'd been thinking about for three months, reliving the kisses they'd shared at the Winter Palace, plus all the other embraces they'd had in that time.

With the door to the bedroom closed behind them, shutting out the rest of the world and cocooning them in their own little nest of lust and desire, Luka smiled at her. After encircling her waist, he brought their bodies together, forcing a whimper from her as he placed warm, wet kisses along her throat. She buried her hands in his blond hair, doing her best to hold onto him as her knees buckled.

"I've dreamt of having you naked in my bed," he whispered against her heated skin.

Inhaling, she filled her lungs with enough air to say, "Then we should do our best to fulfill those dreams, my love."

He blew a puff of air over the sensitive skin behind her ear and she shivered. "I will play your lady's maid tonight."

While he removed her clothes, his touch was gentle and intoxicating by its very innocent nature. Vera grew frustrated because he wouldn't caress or tease any part of her body. Luka seemed more focused on getting her naked than anything else.

"Why will you not touch me?" she asked as he urged her to sit on the edge of the bed. She wore only her stockings and her slippers. He'd laid the rest of her clothing over the back of a chair to keep them from wrinkling.

Luka knelt in front of her then slid his hands up her calves to her knees where he encouraged her to spread her thighs. She did so before she realized how exposed she would be to his gaze.

"I wish to taste your desire first, then touching will come," he muttered, moving close enough to her to be able to run his fingers through the curls that covered her mound.

"Oh" was all she could think of to say. All other thoughts fled her mind when he leaned forward to place a kiss at her most private center. He used his fingers to reveal the little button of flesh she'd discovered could bring her joy when touched. Only he flicked it with the tip of his tongue then licked it.

She almost levitated off the mattress at that intimate of a caress. Her other lover had never used his mouth on her like that. Obviously he wasn't the great lover she'd thought he'd been. Luka began to suckle on her, drawing a moan from Vera.

Not knowing what to do with her hands, she twisted them in the blankets under her, but Luka pulled away and chuckled at her protest.

"Touch your breasts, Vera. Learn what makes you excited," he ordered.

"Your mouth on me like that does it," she admitted, not ashamed to confess that to him in the dark.

"I know. You're wet." He rubbed his thumbs over her inner flesh, enticing her to rock her hips toward him.

"Please." She wasn't entirely sure what she was asking for at that moment. Did she want more of his mouth or did she want him inside her? Something told her that making love to Luka was going to be far better than any other man she'd ever shared her body with.

"In good time, Vera. First, we will give you pleasure, then I'll take mine."

He dove back down and she cried out when he stabbed his tongue inside her. Then he eased his fingers beside it to entice and drive her need higher and higher until she thought she would explode because of the pressure.

She cupped her breasts, squeezing them hard for a second before softening her grip. Vera licked her fingertips then pinched her nipples between finger and thumb. She twisted just a little and the hint of pain shot through her to pool in her pussy. Luka hummed in approval as she grew wetter.

"Luka, I need," she whined, knowing exactly what she wanted, but not sure he'd give it to her this time. "I want you inside me."

Vera squeaked when Luka surged to his feet. Her cheeks heated when he stared down at her and she envisioned how wanton she must look, sprawled on the comforters, cradling her breasts while her legs were spread open and her curls glistening with his spit.

"Beautiful." He growled as he ripped open his trousers then shoved them along with his underthings down to his knees.

She smiled when he grabbed her legs to wrap them around his waist, positioning his shaft at her opening.

Their moans mingled in the air around them as he sank into her. Arching, Vera absorbed the fullness and thickness of his flesh invading her. Luka didn't stop until he was buried to the hilt. She shuddered and tightened her legs, bringing him as close as she could.

He took her hips in his hands then started to stroke in and out. Vera let her hands drop to the silk under her, holding on to it the best she could even though she slid back and forth in rhythm with Luka.

"Amazing." He grunted as she clenched her inner muscles. He peeled one of his hands from her waist before reaching between her thighs to taking her clit between his fingers. He tugged, rubbed and did his best to drive her crazy.

Vera's orgasm burst through her and she cried out as lust overwhelmed her. Her eyes rolled back in her head. She was sure her heart stopped for a moment as well. It started up again when Luka pulled out. Propping herself up on her elbows, she watched as he pumped his shaft once then twice.

She gasped as the hot liquid spurting from his rod spilled onto her stomach. He fell forward, catching himself with his clean hand right before he crushed her. Vera wasn't sure what to think about the mess he'd made, but she barely touched the cross-shaped brand on his cheek in thanks.

He jerked away from her almost like she'd burnt him. Vera let her hand drop and tried to keep from feeling hurt, though she should've known better. Luka had never allowed her to touch his scar since they'd met. There was something about it that caused him pain. She didn't know if it was physical or emotional, but she thought they'd grown close enough that it wouldn't matter if she touched him or not.

Luka straightened before pulling his trousers up to be able to move easier. She watched as he strolled over to the dresser where a pitcher sat. He took one of the clothes then dampened it. After washing, he rinsed the cloth before turning back to her. He cleaned off her stomach without saying a word.

Vera kept silent, not sure what to do. With her other lovers, they would sneak out of her room before anyone could catch them together. She wondered if Luka expected her to leave.

"Stay there," he ordered. "Let me get undressed then I'll finish getting your stockings off."

Blushing, Vera realized she still wore those and her slippers. She'd never gotten so caught up in love making that she'd forgotten to get completely naked. It seemed rather wanton, yet Luka didn't look bothered by her eagerness at all. In fact, he hadn't even taken any of his own clothes off before he'd made love to her.

She didn't wait for him to remove the rest of her items, doing it herself before she slid under the covers to settle against the pillows. Vera watched as Luka took his time revealing his body to her. His broad shoulders and chest tapered down to a narrow waist. He was muscular, and she wondered if he enjoyed outdoor activities or if he boxed or fenced at one of the gentleman clubs in the city.

When he turned and caught her staring, he smirked. "Like what you see, love?"

"Oh yes," she breathed. Her gaze dropped to his shaft where it laid semi-hard against his thigh.

Luka chuckled as he walked over to join her. He wrapped his arms around her, pulling her back against his chest. He pushed her curls out of the way then nipped the nape of her neck. "I think we should rest a little then see what else we can get up to."

He tucked one of his arms under the pillows while covering her stomach with his other hand. She entwined their fingers.

"May I ask you something?"

Vera wasn't sure if his grunt meant yes or no, so she decided to ask anyway. "Why did you spill on my stomach instead of inside me?"

"Do you wish to become with child?"

She shook her head. "Not at the moment, especially since we're not married."

His chin brushed the back of her hair, so she assumed he was nodding. "That was the only way I have of protecting you at this moment."

"Thank you," she murmured.

Luka didn't respond and his deep breathing informed her that he'd fallen asleep. Smiling, Vera snuggled closer to him, looking forward to what would happen next.

Chapter Six

Petrograd, Russia
June 1918

So the rumors were true. Lucifer strolled along the street, keeping his head down while trying to get to Vera's aunt's house before anyone noticed him. He wasn't afraid for his life or anything like that, since the mortals couldn't kill him. He simply wanted to be out of the way when everything exploded.

A civil war was going to break out, as far as Lucifer could tell, and he was accomplished enough to read the tides of anger and frustration running through Petrograd. The Bolsheviks promised "Peace! Land! Bread!" to the people who supported them. Well, the war-weary Russians got their peace, but there was no bread for people to eat and no land for the returning soldiers to work.

Tsar Nicholas had abdicated the throne in March of 1917, then the Bolsheviks had taken over from the Provincial Government in October of that same year. So much confusion, and no matter how well-meaning they were, the Bolsheviks were starting to see how discord and unfulfilled promises could tear a country apart.

The Romanovs were under house arrest at the Alexander Palace, but Lucifer feared for them as much as he did for Vera and the other nobles. There might not be titles and grand estates any more, but there was still a great deal of hatred and resentment toward the privileged few who had ruled over Russia for generations.

Sounds of shouting came from ahead of him, and Lucifer sped up, hoping and praying that he would get to Vera before the mob did. He had horrible flashbacks to the French Revolution where nobles were guillotined in the streets for being nothing more than obnoxious and wealthier than their poorer counterparts.

He'd been helpless to take care of all of them back then. Though he had snuck a few of them out of the country into England, the ones he hadn't been able to save would always haunt him. He wasn't going to add Vera's ghost to the crowd living in his memories.

After skidding to a stop at the corner of Vera's street, he peered around the edge of the shop. There was a mob of ragged men milling around. Lucifer could smell alcohol and knew they were drinking to build up their courage to do something violent. He needed to go through them to get to the woman he loved.

Lucifer glanced down at the clothes he wore, snorting when he realized he would stick out like a thoroughbred among a herd of donkeys. He tried using his power to hide his presence, but like there had been earlier, there was an emptiness inside where his power used to be. He'd discovered it when he'd sought to go directly to the Palen mansion. He'd have been worried about its absence if he wasn't so wrapped up in saving Vera.

He tore off his wool overcoat, dumping it in a trash bin then stripped off his jacket and vest, tossing them in with his coat. Jerking on his shirt, he tore holes in the fabric before crouching down to grab handfuls of dirt to rub onto the pristine white surface. Lucifer made sure to get some on his face and pants.

After scuffing up his shoes to take some of the shine off, he headed down the street, lurching from side to side as though he'd been drinking as well. He tried not to make too much eye contact with anyone, not wanting to get dragged into what was about to happen.

Lucifer did keep track of his progress as he stumbled through the crowd and when he got abreast of the gates to the countess's house, he drove into it, forcing it open then slamming it shut behind him before anyone else could follow.

He pounded on the door. "Vera, open up. It's Luka."

It seemed like centuries before he heard the locks being turned then the door was thrown open. He shoved his way into the foyer where he found Vera, Svetlana and a few other people.

"Oh thank goodness, Luka. Are you okay?" Vera threw herself into his arms.

Embracing her, he buried his face into her curls and breathed deep. Everything inside him relaxed when her familiar scent filled his nose. "I'm fine. I had to get dirty to be able to get past the men outside. You need to pack right now. I have to figure a way to get you all out of the city."

"I sent the girls to my sister's in London a couple of weeks ago," Svetlana told him. "I had a feeling something like this would happen."

"Good. Who will be coming with you?" He glanced at the two maids and the footman who stood slightly to the side. "Do you wish to leave or will you be staying?"

The footman glared at him. "I'll be staying. I won't run if it comes to a fight for my country."

"I'm glad for your courage," Lucifer told him. "I hold no allegiance to this country, so I won't be fighting. I'll be running and if you think that makes me a coward then so be it. I'll be a living coward while you'll be dead within a month." He pointed to the door. "Now get out of here. You're of no more use to me."

The females gasped as the footman tore off his uniform coat then threw it to the ground before spitting on it. Lucifer didn't react, his mind already on the next problem. He looked at the maids.

"Are you staying or going?"

"We're going," they said at the same time.

"Okay. So I have to figure out passage for four women," he muttered, pacing in the foyer. He worked the logistics through his mind, not paying attention to the fact that none of the ladies had moved.

"Aren't you coming with us, Luka?"

Lucifer jerked to a stop and stared at them. "Why are you still standing here? Go pack, but remember you can't take every dress or pair of shoes. You must pack light and make sure you hide any jewels you wish to take with you. If you don't hide them well, they'll be stolen or confiscated. I wish I had more time to plan this, but things are going to explode tonight. Not just here in Petrograd, but throughout Russia." He cradled Vera's face in his hand. "When the dust settles, this country won't resemble the one you knew. I've seen this before in other places in the world."

Fear hid deep under the surface of her eyes, but she nodded. Lucifer let her go then stepped back. He gestured toward the stairs.

"Now go."

The women raced upstairs as best they could in their dresses.

"Wait." He paused until they were all looking at him. "Put on the plainest dresses you have. I don't want anything that will mark you as any different than the other women wandering the streets tonight."

While they packed, Lucifer went through the rooms on the ground floor. He found some silverware he could pawn for some ready cash. He would have to get them to his new apartment—it was one he'd set up shortly after the Bolsheviks had taken power. It wasn't in his name and he'd paid cash for it. Nothing about it said a man of wealth lived there. He'd done his best to look as disreputable as possible each time he'd visited.

Even before the revolutions in 1917, he'd been slowly emptying his Russian bank accounts, moving money into accounts out of the country. Also, he'd been liquidating a lot of his assets in country and he'd stashed emergency money in his apartment.

Lucifer had planned on talking Vera into leaving Russia and going to London with him. He would've even married her, if that was what it would take to get her away from Petrograd, but now that wasn't an option. The only choice he had was smuggling them out of the city.

He closed his eyes, picturing a map of Russia and the closest countries. Most of them had been affected by the war that was still being fought on the continent, but he thought if he could at least get the women to Helsinki in Finland, they would have a chance to get to London to join up with the rest of Svetlana's family.

He'd make sure they had plenty of money to help them on their way.

"This would be so much easier if I had my powers," he muttered, shoving his hands through his hair. "What happened to them? With as much rage and fear boiling up around here, I should be beyond full."

"Who are you talking to, Luka?"

Whipping around, he saw Vera and Svetlana standing in the doorway of the room. He grimaced after checking out their clothes. While they might be the plainest dresses they had, they were certainly of far better quality than those of the maids who joined them. There was no way either Vera or her aunt would be able to fit into the maids' clothing, so they would have to deal with what they had.

"Just muttering to myself, love." He forced a smile that he didn't feel, hoping it gave them a little confidence. "I think I know what we have to do, but it involves going to my apartment on the other side of Petrograd."

"Apartment? Your house is only a block from here," Vera pointed out.

He took their bags, wincing at the weight of them. "I hope these are weighed down by jewels and things you can sell, and not by shoes."

"Of course we didn't pack any shoes." Svetlana glared at him, obviously affronted that he would suggest that. "We know the dangers, Luka. We packed our jewelry and a few other items that could be used as bribes."

"Speaking of which..." He pulled the silverware from his pockets before splitting it up to hand to each of the maids. "Here. You might end up needing these."

They hesitated and looked at Svetlana for permission. Lucifer shook the forks at them.

"It's a different world out there, ladies. Nothing is ever going to be the same. You must make this decision on your own."

After his little speech, both maids threw back their shoulders and took the silver. Svetlana didn't protest, even though Lucifer was pretty sure it had been a family heirloom. When they were done stuffing it in their own packs, he looked them all over and sighed.

God, if you're looking out for the mortals you professed to love so much, then here's your chance to show me how much you care. Help me get these ladies safely out of the city before all hell breaks loose. He didn't know if his prayer got through or not, but all he could do was hope God heard him.

If only Mika'il could see him now, the archangel would be astonished to see Lucifer actually helping mortals escape.

"Okay. We'll go out the kitchen door and through the back courtyard. Hopefully, the mobs won't have got that far yet. Once we get out on the streets, don't talk to anyone or even look at any of them. They'll know within seconds you're upper class. There's nothing we can do about that."

"Luka, what apartment are you talking about?" Vera grabbed a hold of his arm, pulling him to a stop.

He took a deep breath, not wanting to get into a discussion about his activities right then, but knowing she wouldn't let it go. "Before the abdication and the Bolsheviks taking over, I had started planning to leave Russia. My instincts were telling me that something like this would happen and I didn't want to be here when it did. I wasn't worried about money or business interests. Many people will die because of this, Vera, and I wasn't going to be caught in the middle of it."

She blinked and before she could ask the question he saw in her eyes, he told her, "I was going to ask you to marry me then move us both to London. With the war going on, I figured it would end up being safer there than here."

"You were?" Her bright smile blinded him.

"I might be a rather self-centered and arrogant bastard, but I love you, Vera. I wasn't going to leave you behind."

If any of the fallen who feared him could have heard him tell a mortal he loved her, they probably would've passed out from shock. In the millennia he'd existed on earth, he'd never been in love with any woman he'd slept with. He would sleep with them then move on.

Vera had touched his heart from the very beginning and after spending so much time with her, he'd discovered he cared deeply for her.

"I love you too, Luka." She kissed him.

As much as he would've loved to keep on kissing her, then carry her upstairs to make love in her bed, he knew they couldn't do it. Danger grew with every minute they wasted.

The shattering of glass broke them apart, and he shot a look toward the front of the house. "The mob has gathered their courage. We need to get out now."

He herded the women in the direction of the kitchen, stopping them before any stepped outside. "Let me check to make sure no one has got into the garden."

Glancing around, he spotted a large carving knife lying on one of the counters. He grabbed it then slowly opened the door. He slid out, leaving the door open a few inches. After searching the entire area, he waved for his group to join him.

The ladies scurried across the yard to where he stood at the gate leading into the alley on the other side of the block the house sat on. They repeated the sequence and once they were out on the streets, winding their way through the city. Lucifer tried not to go too fast, not wanting to lose any of his ladies.

The city exploded around them as the tension ignited. Yelling, fighting and gunshots rang on the streets. They dodged from doorway to doorway as they tried to avoid the gangs fighting with each other. Lucifer kept hold of Vera's hand and dragged her behind him. Ultimately, she was the only one he wanted to save. If it came to down to it, he would sacrifice the other women to keep Vera alive and with him.

Chapter Seven

Petrograd, Russia
June 1918

Bending over, Vera pressed her hand to her right side. "Luka, we have to stop and rest."

Luka paused, motioning to her and the others to take a break. "We should be all right at the moment. They'll have headed toward the palace and the sections of Petrograd where the stores are. They're looking for food and things to steal so they can sell them."

"Who is fighting exactly?" Svetlana asked, keeping her voice low.

"The main groups are the liberals and monarchists— people who are against the Bolsheviks—and the Soviets. They are fighting for rule of the country because what the Soviets promised hasn't happened yet." He paused for a second then continued, "Well, they did promise to leave the war, which they did, but all those soldiers need jobs and food to eat. There are no jobs to be had now that the war effort is over for Russia."

Vera nodded. She'd read the news articles about the poor soldiers and their families starving in the streets of Moscow and Petrograd. There had been such hope when the tsar had abdicated, yet she privately thought the problems hadn't been fixed simply because Nicholas was no longer ruling Russia.

"It makes sense, but why kill each other? Why can't they sit and talk about what they want to do?"

Luka snorted and laughed. "Because compromising would be seen as a weakness. Lenin believes his views are the only way Russia will survive. He's unwilling to listen to anyone else, whether their ideas are sound or not. He was the one who brought about the October Revolution and he is one of the reasons why Russia is going to be plunged into a civil war."

She straightened then checked with her aunt and their maids. When the three ladies nodded, she met Luka's questioning gaze. "We're ready to go."

"Good. We've only a few more blocks to go. I'll grab my bags then we'll head to the harbor. Thank goodness, it isn't far from here."

He took off again and she did her best to stay with him. Vera didn't know how he managed not to tire like the rest of them. It was as though he didn't get fatigued. He moved so confidently even while skulking from doorway to doorway. The strange thing for her was that she never doubted the fact that he would get them safely out of Petrograd. Vera couldn't say how she knew that and it didn't matter. She would follow him anywhere he led.

"Here we are. Come with me." Luka entered a rundown building and the ladies went with him.

There wasn't anyone at the front desk, so no one stopped them as they climbed the stairs to the third floor. Luka opened a door then motioned for her to go in. When she stepped into the one room apartment, she hesitated. The space was empty of anything except three large bags. Luka grabbed a shirt and pants from one of them.

"Turn around, everyone. I'm going to change then we'll leave," he told them.

"Where is all your furniture? What happened to your house?" She didn't understand. It had been several months since she'd seen him. Luka often left the city to travel for his business ventures, so she'd never thought to ask him why she'd never visited his home.

"I abandoned it about four months ago. There's nothing there that I'm attached to. I can buy new things when we get to Paris," Luka told her as he changed.

She watched as he dropped his dirty clothes to the floor then put the clean ones on. "You really have been planning this for a while, haven't you?"

"Not much catches me by surprise, Vera. I could see all of the trouble coming. When the Bolsheviks took power, I had already transferred most of my money into banks elsewhere in the world. They couldn't confiscate what they couldn't get their hands on." He gestured to the three bags. "Those are my only concrete possessions."

"What's in them?"

He swept up all three then slung a bag over each shoulder while carrying the third. He also picked up hers and Svetlana's as well. "Let's go. When we leave the building, take a right. Remember we want to get to the harbor. We'll either find a captain that will take us to Helsinki or we'll buy a boat and navigate there ourselves."

They left the building and the trip to the harbor was just as harrowing as their flight from Svetlana's house had been. There were a few times when she thought they would be robbed or taken captive, but Luka always managed to get them safely away without violence or trouble.

Finding a captain willing to take them to Finland was another problem, and Vera stood watching as Luka got increasingly frustrated with the men who refused him. It was as thought he'd never been told no before. Finally, she stepped in. While traveling the world with her parents, she'd learnt how to negotiate with people.

She still wasn't able to find one who would take them himself, but she did find one who was willing to sell his small boat to them. When she told Luka the amount, he didn't blink as he simply opened one of his bags then grabbed three handfuls of stacked rubles. He handed them to the captain and they shook on the deal.

"Do you know how to sail?" she asked as they climbed onto the boat.

He showed them where to stash their bags then launched it from the dock. "I have sailed far bigger ships than this one over far rougher seas than we'll be experiencing. Have no fear, Vera, my love, I'll get you to Finland and safety."

"I do trust you," she whispered before pushing up on her toes to kiss him.

They couldn't do any more than that. Luka wanted to get out into the Gulf of Finland before anyone with authority noticed the boat leaving. He was sure the dock had been closed and the sailors weren't supposed to leave port until they were allowed to go.

Svetlana and the maids sat on the bottom, leaning against each other while trying to catch their breath. Vera stood at the back of the boat and watched the city of Petrograd disappear from view.

"Do you think Alexandra and the girls will be all right?" she asked, but didn't look at Luka because she didn't want to see the truth in his gaze. She saw him shrug from out of the corner of her eye.

"I can't say for sure, but I think it would be the wrong move to make to kill a tsar and his family, especially one connected to pretty much every royal family in Europe."

His reasoning was sound, but somehow she didn't feel reassured. No one had thought Rasputin could be killed, yet they'd assassinated him in 1916, proving that not even a holy man was exempt from death.

"Will we ever come back here?"

Luka grunted then said, "I don't know. It would have to be a different city if I were to ever return. I don't like Lenin's philosophy and beliefs, and I think he and his Soviets will win this war. Maybe one day things will change and we'll be able to walk the streets of Petrograd again. Maybe even dance in the ballroom at the Winter Palace."

She went to stand by his side, staring out into the darkness of the gulf. "Do you really believe that?"

He slid one hand underneath her curls to cup the back of her head. She shuddered at the warmth of his touch as he ducked slightly to meet her gaze.

"There aren't many things I believe in anymore, Vera, but I do believe that. We will come back here and dance together." He kissed her hard before turning back to the wheel.

* * * *

She lost track of how long it took them to get to Helsinki and freedom. All she knew was that Luka never slept. Whenever she woke up from her fitful naps, he'd be standing at the wheel, steering them over the water to a new life. Knowing he had been willing to ask her to marry him brought joy to her heart, though she wasn't sure she could say yes if he asked her right then.

Vera needed to find her parents and make sure they were okay. They had gone to England to stay with some relatives before all the upheaval. She would do what she could to get Svetlana reunited with her daughters while doing her best not to cling to Luka. From a comment he'd made when they were in Petrograd, she had a feeling he wouldn't be accompanying them to England.

"We're here." Luka nodded ahead of him.

After pushing to her feet, she cried out in relief to see the large harbor of Helsinki unfold in front of them. Once they'd docked, it was another long and arduous tangle to get someone to allow them to enter the country without papers, but Luka again reached into his magical bank bag and pulled out enough Finnish *markkas* to bribe everyone they talked to.

Several hours after arriving in Helsinki, they were checking into a hotel several blocks from the harbor. Luka got two rooms then looked at her.

"Will you share my bed tonight?"

Vera nodded. "Of course I will."

Svetlana didn't say a word when they parted ways. They were on the same floor, but their room was several doors down from Svetlana and the maids.

Luka had offered to give them some money so they could leave if they wished. Both maids stated they had nowhere to go, no family, so they would continue traveling with Vera and Svetlana.

When the door shut behind her, Vera dropped her bag then threw herself into Luka's arms. He crushed her to him before taking her mouth in demanding fashion. She gasped at the firm grip he had on her butt.

They broke apart, chests heaving, and Luka looked over at the bathroom.

"Why don't we get clean then we can continue this?"

It sounded like the best plan in the world to Vera. She wanted to wash off the stench of her fear and get a fresh start at this new life she'd found herself in. Luka helped with her clothes, leaving them in a pile on the floor. When she picked them up to toss over the chair, he smiled.

"I don't want them wrinkled. I do have to wear them tomorrow," she informed him.

"You and Svetlana can go out with the other two and buy some other clothes." He gestured toward his bags. "I'll make sure you have money."

Vera wanted to make a comment about his magic bag of money, but when he held out his hand to her with a slight leer on his face, she forgot.

The bath wasn't very big. She wasn't going to complain about being pressed against Luka's wet body for the duration. He ran the cloth all over her skin, washing the dirt off her.

"Spread your legs," he commanded.

Leaning back against his chest, she did as he told her. The rough cloth against her sensitive inner thighs caused her to shiver. When Luka reached the junction of her legs, he rubbed her clit and Vera whimpered.

"Do you like that?" he whispered into her ear before he nibbled on it.

When he'd washed her body, he helped her out of the bathtub then toweled her dry. After sweeping her into his arms, he carried her to the bed where he laid her down. He slipped his hand between her thighs again.

She couldn't get a sound out as he touched and teased, rubbing hard on her flesh until she was rocking into his touch. Vera wanted more. She needed more.

"Luka," she pleaded.

"Hush, love." He lifted her up then helped her turn around to straddle his hips.

Vera let her head fall back as she impaled herself on his shaft. She cried out when he filled her completely and she froze, trying to calm her breathing so she could adjust to him being inside her.

"Are you all right?" Luka stroked his hands down her sides to grip her hips.

"Yes. Just taking a second to get used to you."

She braced her hands on Luka's chest then rose up, letting him slide almost all the way out. Taking a deep breath, she took him in again. Once she'd relaxed around his shaft, Luka took over. His fingers bit into her flesh and she knew she'd have bruises tomorrow. Not that she cared.

Their rhythm began to speed up until the sound of skin against skin filled the room. Vera couldn't catch her breath as she rode Luka, clenching her inner muscles to massage Luka's length. She wanted to shove Luka over the edge.

Suddenly, he wrapped his arms around her waist then flipped them over. She gasped then moaned as he drove into her deeper and harder. While bracing one of his hands by her head, Luka slipped one in between them so he could caress the hard nub of flesh hidden by her soft folds. After leaning down, he bit her gently on the shoulder.

"Luka." Vera groaned as all those sensations coalesced and exploded inside her. Pleasure rocketed over her body, causing her to tremble and cry out.

All of her shivering and tensing seemed to draw Luka's own climax out, but at the last moment, Luka pulled out and spilled his seed all over her stomach again. A burning disappointment tore through Vera for a mere second. The thought that if he had emptied himself inside her she might have got with child didn't bother her as much as it probably should have.

The faint feeling that she might not see him once she left Finland was stronger now than ever before. Luka flopped to the side and Vera rested her hand on his chest, needing to keep in contact with him.

"Every time it gets better," Luka muttered and he rolled over to look at her. "Each time I lose a little more of myself to you."

"Is that such a bad thing?" she had to ask, even if she might not like the answer.

He sighed then pursed his lips while he thought. "Before I met you, I would say yes and that something like this would never happen to me. I wasn't looking for any kind of commitment. My life isn't conducive to attachments. I'm not the type of person who puts other people's concerns before mine."

"Yet you came to find me, Luka. If you were the man you described, you would've left Petrograd without a backward glance, not got us out of there." She trailed her fingers over the ridges of his stomach.

Grunting, Luka didn't answer here as he climbed out of bed to pad over to the bathroom. She heard the rush of water and imagined he was cleaning off. The itch of his spend on her skin annoyed her, causing her to contemplate following him. Before she could sit up, Luka returned with a damp cloth.

Vera blushed a little when he washed her stomach and between her thighs. "Thank you," she said softly.

His smile touched her heart, bringing tears to her eyes. She blinked them away. No man liked a weeping woman and she wasn't about to irritate him before he disappeared from her life.

After tossing the cloth in the sink, Luka came back to climb beside her under the covers. He pulled her back against his chest, surrounding her with his body. Vera sighed, feeling safe for the first time since Luka had shown up on Svetlana's doorstep and the riots had started.

"What do you think is happening at home?" she whispered.

Luka's hot breath bathed her neck as he exhaled. "I think they're tearing your country apart. It might have just started, but it's not going to end as quickly. Many will die before this is over."

Tears welled in her eyes again, but this time it was sadness that filled her. "If I ever go back, it'll never be the same."

"No it won't, and I'm sorry for that. I know what it's like to be exiled from your home, to know you'll never see the things you used to love again."

Wiggling around, she turned to face him. "Where is your home? You've never talked about it."

Luka opened his eyes to meet hers and the desolation in their dark depths made her breath catch in her throat. She touched his cheek where the scar marred his skin.

"When did you get this?"

"When I was exiled from my home. I disobeyed my father and rebelled against his rule. So I was tossed away like garbage, even though what I did was for the good of the people."

"Were you a prince?" she teased.

"Yes, I was considered a prince amongst my people, yet it didn't matter when it came to my punishment." Luka nuzzled her palm. "Since then, I haven't thought much about it. You've filled my heart and mind with other things, Vera. If nothing else, I owe you my gratitude for that."

"I don't want your gratitude, Luka. I just want your heart. Will you give it to me?"

Maybe it was bold of her to ask, but she wasn't going to let him leave her without some kind of declaration.

Chuckling, Luka grabbed her hand then pressed it to his chest right over where his heart was. "Love, I was ready to ask you to marry me, and trust me when I say that's never happened before. I've never met a woman I wanted to spend my life with. You have my heart and everything else that is mine."

She realized he hadn't answered her question about where his home was, but she decided it didn't matter. It was obvious he was never going back there, so she would make a home for him wherever she ended up. She would give him a reason to return to her.

"Do you feel the same?" There was hesitation and nervousness in his voice.

Vera put all of her love for him in her kiss as she merged their lips. There were promises and dreams mingled with happiness and joy in their embrace. Once she broke away, she snuggled close to him.

"You'll come back to me," she murmured as she let her eyes drift close.

"I'll always come back to you. You're my home now, Vera."

Luka's soft vow chased her into her dreams.

Chapter Eight

As the sun filtered through the curtains the next morning, Vera reached out to touch Luka, but her hand landed on a cool pillow instead. She pushed up to search the room with her gaze. She was alone.

Where had Luka gone? As she started to panic, she noticed a white sheet of paper lying on the nightstand next to her. After snatching it up, she was relieved to see it was from Luka.

Off to arrange passage for you to England. Also, Svetlana will be stopping by. The four of you need to go shopping for some new clothes. I left some markkas on the table for you. I'll see you around noon. Love Luka.

She flopped back and clasped the paper to her heart. He hadn't left her. Yet she still had a faint apprehension that he wasn't going to London with them after all. Would this short time in Finland be the last time she saw him?

Shaking her head, she remembered what he'd told her last night.

"I'll always come back to you. You're my home now, Vera."

She and Svetlana would go to England and try to contact Vera's parents and Svetlana's daughters. Once that happened, Vera would set up a home to give Luka something to return to. She would wait as long as it took for him to come back.

A knock on the door got her out of bed. She wrapped the comforter around her body before she went to answer it. Peering around the edge, she saw Svetlana and the two maids standing there.

"Luka said we were to come and get you. We'll have breakfast downstairs then he's arranged for us to go shopping for some clothes." Svetlana eyed her. "I see you just woke up."

"Yes." After stepping back, she waved for them to enter. "Give me ten minutes and I'll be ready to go."

Svetlana waved her hand dismissively. "Take your time. I'm sure we won't be leaving until tomorrow at the earliest. Do you want one of the maids to stay with you to help you dress? I'll go down and order some tea and breakfast for us."

"You can all go down. It won't take me long."

Her aunt nodded. "All right. We'll see you in twenty minutes or so."

Vera shut the door before going into the bathroom to wash. Once that was done, she dressed quickly, eager for something to eat and some different clothes. She wrinkled her nose at the stiffness of the salt-water splattered fabric. Vera grabbed her bag then stuffed the *markkas* into it. Her room key went in as well after she'd locked the door.

When she got to the lobby, she found Svetlana and the maids seated at a table in the hotel restaurant. Tea and breakfast had just arrived, so Vera took her place before dishing up her food. She didn't mind the presence of the two young ladies who worked for them. Things were changing throughout the world, and society was going to have to learn how to deal with them.

"Do you know where we're supposed to go to get clothes?" she asked after taking a sip.

"His lordship said he would have a carriage arranged for us. We need to go to the front desk and enquire about it," one of the maids, Ariana, said.

Vera's mind was on what Luka was doing and what was happening back in Russia.

"Thank you, Ariana. When you're finished eating, would you be willing to go and take care of that for us?" Vera didn't command her to do it. No reason to be demanding now when Ariana and Rosa could leave them any time they wanted.

"Yes, ma'am." Ariana smiled, her pleasure at being asked obvious.

"What about money? I'm not sure we have enough to get outfits for all of us." Svetlana took a dainty bite of eggs.

Vera fought the need to roll her eyes. "Don't worry about that, Aunt. Luka has left us more than enough to get a couple of outfits each. We won't be able to go to a seamstress though. There's no time to get new wardrobes done."

"But—" Her aunt started to protest, but Vera shook her head.

"Luka will try to get us on our way as soon as possible." She gestured toward the harbor. "As the situation gets worse in Petrograd and the rest of the country, more people will be trying to use Helsinki as a place of safety. Also, they'll want to go to other places on the continent, even with the war going on.

We need to be out of here before that happens or we won't be able to go."

Svetlana frowned and Vera knew her aunt wasn't happy about everything, yet there was nothing they could do about the situation. Ariana went to the front desk while the other three finished their meals.

Once they were done, Ariana led the way outside where a carriage waited to take them to the closest dress shop. Vera helped the two maids to pick out two dresses each along with new underthings and shoes. Aunt Svetlana didn't look happy about the quality of the dresses she was given as choices, but Vera reminded her that they didn't have much time, so getting new, more elaborate ones wasn't possible.

It was noon by the time the ladies were done shopping, and Luka strolled in as Vera was paying and arranging to have the clothing delivered to the hotel. He bowed at Svetlana before greeting Vera with a quick kiss.

"Were you able to find everything you needed?" he asked as he escorted them from the shop. He flagged down a carriage. "I'll take us all out for lunch while I tell you what I've planned for you."

"Yes, we got everything we need for the trip. I'm sure we'll be able to get more things once we're in England," Vera said as she climbed into the carriage followed by the others.

Luka told the driver where to take them then settled next to Vera in the seat facing forward along with Svetlana. Ariana and Rosa sat with their backs to the driver.

"You had enough money then?"

Vera nodded. "More than enough. So when do we leave?"

Luka smiled. "Wait until we're at the restaurant, love. We'll arrange everything then."

She pushed aside her eagerness, wishing to know right then and there where they were going and how, but knew Luka wasn't going to say anything until he was ready. So she leaned against him while they rode through the city to the restaurant, listening as Luka drew out the maids and she learnt more about them than she'd ever known before.

Ariana had just turned twenty and had come to work for Svetlana two years ago. She seemed like an intelligent girl who didn't want to be a maid all of her life, though Vera admitted it would've been hard for Ariana to move beyond that role if they had stayed in Russia. Maybe in England, she'd have a better shot at her own shop.

Rosa was only eighteen, but like Ariana, she had worked for Vera's aunt for two years. She was quieter and seemed content to be a maid. Both girls were orphans, and Vera found herself planning on doing what she could to either keep them working for her or maybe getting Ariana the shop she wanted.

A few minutes later, they'd arrived and when they were seated, Luka ordered for everyone. Vera noticed he spoke perfect Finnish, which didn't surprise her that much since she knew he did business in several different countries.

When the waiter left, she asked, "When do we leave?"

"We were lucky. There's a ship leaving tomorrow afternoon, heading for Newcastle. You'll disembark there and take the train to London, or wherever your parents are. I'm sure you can get a hold of them as soon as you dock."

"We'll go to London and join up with my girls then find Vera's family," Svetlana spoke up, obviously feeling the need to exert her authority over something.

"Actually, that might be the best idea," Luka said graciously.

Vera reached under the table to squeeze his knee. "Thank you for all your work to help us."

"I also hired two men to go with you as guards. They won't bother you," Luka informed them.

"Strange men? How do you know they won't turn and murder us in our beds as soon as we're alone?" Svetlana pressed her hand to her chest in abject horror.

The smile on Luka's face was pure evil for a spilt second and Vera shivered in fear at that moment. "They know what I would do to them if anything were to happen to you."

Then his face went back to its normal arrogant smirk and Vera wondered what other secrets Luka hid under his smooth veneer. When he covered her hand with his, Vera's fear disappeared. He might be more than she'd thought at first, but he would never hurt her and Vera knew that down to her soul.

"They'll escort you to London and stay until you rejoin your father."

Their food arrived and Luka wouldn't say any more until after they'd eaten. It wasn't until they were back at the hotel, sitting in the lobby that Luka resumed telling them the rest.

"Tomorrow morning, we'll head to the docks where you'll board the ship. I got you the best cabins available. You and Svetlana will share one and the girls will have the other. The guards will sleep outside your doors." Luka leaned back in his chair, steepling his fingers as he studied her and the others.

"You're not going with us, are you?" Maybe she should've waited until they were alone before she asked, but her question came out without her thinking.

He glanced at Svetlana, and her aunt stood, gathering Ariana and Rosa with a look.

"I think we should go up to our room and make sure we've packed everything. Come and get us when you wish to have dinner." She walked off before Vera could stop her.

After they had left, Luka pushed to his feet then held out his hand to her. "Why don't we go for a stroll, Vera?"

She didn't want to go. She wanted to go to their room and make love until she convinced Luka not to leave her. Vera took his hand, letting him tuck hers in the crook of his elbow before leading her out onto the pavement. They walked a little ways then Luka sighed.

"You're right. I'm not going with you."

Vera tensed, gripping his arm tight. "Why not? Where are you going?"

Luka urged her closer to him, slipping his arm around her waist. She didn't care about proper distance and lady-like behavior. All she wanted was Luka's strength surrounding her.

"I can't just leave Russia without making sure some people are safe," he murmured as they passed a large group of people.

"Why? You told me you thought no one would hurt them because they were related to a majority of the ruling families on the continent." She kept her voice low, not sure why they were whispering, but figured if Luka wanted to keep it quiet, she would go along with him.

He shrugged. "I'm pretty sure they wouldn't, but I can't help wanting to go back to make sure."

Vera shook her head and smiled. "You say you're arrogant and selfish, Luka, but such a man wouldn't care so much about people. I think you pretend to be a bastard to hide your soft heart."

Luka laughed. "I'm only soft hearted with you, Vera, my love. I don't like most people."

She stopped then pushed up on her toes to press her lips against his ear. "Why don't you take me back to the hotel and show me how much you like me?"

Lust flared in his eyes as he whirled them around to head back in the direction they'd come. "I think that sounds like a great idea."

* * * *

After dressing in one of the new outfits that had been delivered yesterday afternoon, Vera finished packing then looked around the room to make sure she hadn't left anything behind. Luka came in from the hallway.

"The carriage is on its way. Do you have everything?"

"Yes." She turned to look at him. "Is there anything I can do to convince you not to go back?"

He shook his head as he cupped her face in his hands. "I'm sorry, love, but I feel like I need to do this. I haven't been a good person for most of my years on this earth. Maybe you make me want to be better or maybe I'm finally getting it through my head that pouting for years doesn't help anyone. I need to help them and others if I can."

Vera rested her head against his chest for a moment. "I know, Luka, and I love you for it. I just don't want to be without you."

He kissed the top of her head then stepped back. "I have something for you. When you look at it, I hope you think of me until I can come back to you."

He went over to where his bags were sitting. After opening one, he dug through it then pulled something out. Luka gestured for her to sit on the bed before sitting next to her. Her mouth dropped opened when he handed her a small golden egg.

"Where did you get this?" She didn't want to grip it too tightly because she was afraid of breaking it.

"You don't want to know," he told her then sighed. "I took it from the Alexander Palace before the Bolsheviks took over."

"You stole it from the royal family?" Her hands shook as she held the egg up to stare at it.

"Press the diamond in the middle." Luka showed her which one.

Vera couldn't believe she was holding one of the Fabergé eggs. She'd heard about them and that the Romanovs had had the man create such elaborate pieces of artwork. After pushing the jewel, she watched as the egg popped open and a delicate filigree of the Winter Palace appeared. It was so tiny, but beautifully rendered.

"It's amazing, Luka." Vera brushed her lips over Luka's.

"I wanted you to have it, so you would always remember where we first met," he admitted.

"Like I could forget that." She closed the egg then tucked it away in her bag. Then she turned back to wrap her arms around Luka's neck. "Don't wait too long to come back to me. Please."

"I won't. I'll come home to you as soon as I can."

He kissed her and she could almost feel his vow in the depth of his embrace. Luka crushed her to him as though he didn't want to let go of her. Vera said goodbye in that kiss, not wanting to show any emotion while at the dock.

There was a knock on their door and Luka stood to go answer it. Vera brushed the tears off her cheeks as she went to pick up her bag.

"It's time," Luka said from where he stood in the open doorway and Vera saw her aunt and the two maids standing in the hallway.

"All right."

* * * *

Thirty minutes later, they were standing on the dock. Svetlana, Ariana and Rosa had thanked Luka before boarding the ship. Vera stared up into Luka's dark eyes, wishing she could stop the tears, but not even taking several deep breaths helped.

"I know," Luka said softly. He whispered a kiss over her mouth before stepping away. "I'll be back to you before you know it."

"I'll be waiting."

Vera walked up the boarding plank then turned to wave goodbye, but Luka was gone, having slipped into the crowd. Maybe he didn't want to watch her sail away from him. She understood because she hadn't really wished to see him slowly disappear from view as they left the harbor.

"Goodbye," she whispered into the wind.

Chapter Nine

Saint Petersburg, Russia
Present Day

"You just left her in Finland," Mika'il said. "You couldn't escort her to England, stay there and live your own version of happily ever after?"

Lucifer shot to his feet, letting the glass slip from his fingers as he did so. It disappeared before it hit the floor and he started to pace. "I couldn't. I got everything arranged for them, even hired guards to take them all the way to London. They weren't supposed to leave them until she found her parents."

"Do you know if she made it?" Mika'il waved his hand and the liquor vanished along with his glass.

"No. By the time I got to England, over a year had gone by, and I found no trace of her anywhere. I don't understand how that happened. How could I lose one mortal female?" He stuffed his hands in his pockets.

"The same way the Father lost those angels. There is something about them and certain mortals that makes it impossible for us to track them, or figure out where they are in the world. Sometimes it is only with luck that we find them." Mika'il smiled.

Lucifer sent a skeptical look at the archangel. "Do you seriously think it's luck that allows us to find them? Luck is merely God deciding it's time for us to know what he knows."

Mika'il wiggled his head back and forth. "You might be right about that."

"Let's go back out into the ballroom." He had to leave the study. Hell, he wanted to run screaming from the entire palace, but he figured Mika'il would just follow him, so he might as well stay and endure the torture.

"All right."

He led the way back to the ballroom where another group of tourists stood, listening to their guide.

"I went back to Russia after I saw them off," he admitted.

Mika'il frowned. "Why did you do that? You couldn't stay away from a war? Was it the idea of all that hate and pain being there for you to gather and turn into power?"

Lucifer sighed and even he could hear the sadness in that noise. "No. I went back to see if I could save Nicholas and Alexandra. I knew they were going to die, Mika'il. I knew the Soviets couldn't afford to allow them to live and have them be used by the Whites as figureheads for their side."

Mika'il's hand on his arm threw Lucifer off-center. The archangel had gone out of his way to never touch him after the fall. He stared down at the long, tanned fingers on his forearm then looked up into Mika'il's silver eyes.

"You couldn't have saved them, Lucifer. It was their destiny to die that night. There was nothing any of us could've done to stop it." Mika'il clenched his jaw.

"How do you know?"

"Because I wanted to stop it as well. At least stop the children from being killed, but the Father wouldn't allow it. He told me that since I couldn't see the long view of the world, I had to accept his word that their deaths were necessary." Mika'il relaxed a little. "It was one of the few times I wanted to complain to him about the things he makes mortals endure."

Frowning, Lucifer remembered another strange thing that had happened while he was trying to save Vera. "I never did figure out why my powers disappeared the night I got Vera out of Saint Petersburg. It was really the strangest thing, because they came back as soon as I docked at Helsinki."

Mika'il grimaced. "That was probably my fault."

"What do you mean? You can't affect my powers. Only God can take my powers from me. The good thing was that even though I didn't have my powers, I still could function without rest. There has to be something good about being a fallen angel."

"I told him I thought you were abusing them. That you had started the revolutions and you were encouraging the Whites and the Reds to fight." Mika'il cringed at Lucifer's growl. "I might have suggested that he take your powers from you, so you could prove how determined you were to save Vera and the other ladies."

Clenching his hands, Lucifer resisted the urge to slam his fist into Mika'il's face. "I'm not Job, to be played with like a toy in some child's bedroom. I can't believe you hate me that much that you would risk a mortal's life by taking away the only things that could've saved her."

"That's not true." Mika'il poked him in the side. "You saved her without the powers. All of your planning and forward thinking ensured you had contingency routes in place for when the fighting started. I am sorry that I doubted you about that. I might have suggested he take your powers away, but then I told him to give them back as soon as you got across the gulf."

Lucifer couldn't stand near Mika'il any longer. He turned to walk toward a pair of ladies in the middle of the room that had caught his eye the moment he'd stepped back into the ballroom. One stared at her friend with a worried expression on her face while the other lady seemed to be in a trance.

Letting his glamour drop, Lucifer approached them. "Is everything okay, ma'am?"

"I think so. My friend has been acting kind of weird since we got to Saint Petersburg. She keeps telling me she's having *déjà vu*. It's strange too, because she's been right about a lot of things," the worried lady explained to him.

"Maybe she used to live here in a former life," Lucifer suggested. "Reincarnation could explain how she knows those facts."

"Oh, do you think that's what is going on?"

The other woman turned to look at him and shock hit him square in the chest. It was Vera and while she was older, she hadn't changed so much that he didn't recognize her. She had an equally astonished expression on her face.

"I know you," she said, reaching out to touch the scar on his cheek.

Instead of jerking away like he usually did when anyone tried to touch the cross, he let her trace it. "Vera?"

"How do you know my name? We have met before, haven't we? How is that possible?"

Instead of a Russian accent, she had a British one, and Lucifer spotted a few other differences, yet he knew down in the empty place where his soul used to be that it was his Vera returned to him.

"Luka?" Mika'il appeared at his side. "What's wrong?"

"Luka? Your name is Luka Kolwochak. You were made a lord by Tsar Nicholas the second for services rendered to the crown," she murmured, still staring at him. "But that was over a hundred years ago. How could I know any of that?"

"Holy fuck!"

Hearing Mika'il swear was appalling enough that it brought Lucifer out of his stupor. He covered Vera's hand where it still rested on his face then pressed a soft kiss into her palm.

"I'm not sure how it's possible that I've found you after a century of looking. Where have you been? What happened to you? I went to London, looking for you, but there was no trace of you or your parents."

"Umm...what the bloody hell is going on here?" Vera's friend spoke up. "There's no way you two know each other. I'm sure Vera would've told me if she'd ever met a guy who looked like you."

Lucifer shot a pleading look at Mika'il and his former friend sighed.

"I'll take care of this while you try to figure out how all of this happened."

"Luck," Lucifer whispered and the word he spoke caused Mika'il to look a little shell-shocked.

"You might be right." Mika'il flashed a bright smile at the other lady. "Why don't you come with me and I'll explain everything?"

A bit of power behind the wording and the lady walked off with Mika'il like they'd been best friends forever. Vera watched them stroll away before turning back to Lucifer.

"Who are you?" She shook her head. "I really lived here during the final years of the Romanov rule and fled in the middle of the night as civil war broke out?"

He nodded. "My name is Lucifer Daystar. I'm the most powerful fallen angel on earth." He didn't wait for her to say anything in response. "I know that sounds crazy, but it's the truth. That's how I can be here, looking exactly as I did a century ago when we met in a study here at the Winter Palace."

"I was trying to get away from a young man who just wouldn't take no for an answer. You'd been in some kind of meeting." Her hazel eyes studied his face intently. "We kissed that night before we'd even been properly introduced."

Chuckling, he nodded. "Yes. I'm afraid I'm a bit of a rake."

"But I didn't try to stop you, and I know if I had, you would have stopped. I trusted you from the first moment I saw you, which seems odd to me. Especially if you are Lucifer. I should be scared to death of you and running away. I know you sound crazy, but I must be crazy because it makes sense to me. Ever since I could remember, I've wanted to come to Saint Petersburg. It was like a siren's call for me."

Lucifer tucked her hand in the crook of his elbow then began to lead her toward the exit. "I return here often, searching for you, even though I never truly believed I'd be fortunate enough to find you again."

"You found her for me, Lucifer. The last lost angel has come home. Thank you."

The voice of God in his head almost drove him to his knees, but Vera's tight grip on his arm kept him upright.

"Lost angel? Was that voice talking about me?"

After freezing for a second, he met her inquiring gaze. "You heard that?"

She nodded. "Yes. Who was that?"

"It was God, telling me that you were the last one. He's had Mika'il looking for you for millennia. The archangel found his own lost angel last year. He didn't think he'd ever find you."

"He didn't. You did and I'm glad it was you who found me. Would my being an angel explain all these memories I have stored in my brain of all these different lives I swear I lived?"

"Yes." Lucifer escorted her out into one of the many gardens surrounding the Winter Palace. He brought them to a bench then gestured for Vera to sit. "This will seem like a strange question, but do you remember how you died during the life where you lived in Saint Petersburg—or Petrograd, as it was known as back then."

She faced away from him and it was as though he could see her flipping through scenes in her brain like she was watching a slide show. Finally she wrinkled her nose.

"I'm not completely sure, but I think my parents and I died from the Spanish Flu. For some reason, I remember being very sick and somehow knowing I wasn't going to survive."

"That must have been why I couldn't find any trace of you or your parents. It was 1920 before I could make my way back to England. By then, there would be no feel of you left and you probably hadn't been reborn yet." He entwined their fingers then rested their hands on his thigh. "What heart I had left broke the day I realized I would never see you again. It hurt worse than if I had watched you grow older and die."

She rested her head on his shoulder. "I'm sure I'll have a ton of questions eventually, but I just want to sit here and breathe you in. It's as though I finally got that missing piece of my soul back. Do you think you're the reason I kept coming back? Were you what I was searching for each time I returned to earth?"

He shrugged. "I don't know. It might be that you were looking for a way to get back to Heaven. As an angel, you would mourn the loss of your home, even if you didn't know you were such a being."

Suddenly, she swung around to straddle his lap. Vera threaded her fingers through his hair, holding him still as she crushed her lips to his. After gripping her hips, he pulled her tight to him as he relearned the taste of her mouth and the feel of her breasts pressed to his chest.

"You should go get a room," Mika'il suggested silently.

"I'm not ready to talk to you," he warned the archangel.

A soft sigh crossed his mind. *"I know, and I deserve to be on the end of your silent treatment, but I do mean it. Get a room and get reacquainted. We can talk some other time and you can yell at me then for being an ass."*

"Thank you." A vague thought hit him. *"What about Vera's friend?"*

"Bridget and I are old, dear friends of Vera's friend and she just happened to run into us while visiting the Hermitage. So while Vera is meeting an old friend of her own, we are wandering through the art galleries and catching up." Laughter colored Mika'il's words.

Tiffany Aaron

Lucifer sent another silent thank you before cutting off the connection between them. He picked Vera up then set her on her feet. She started to protest, but he placed his finger on her swollen lips.

"I think we should go to my hotel and finish this discussion there," he suggested.

"I agree." She glanced around. "Where did Lydia go?"

"Mika'il and Bridget are wandering the galleries with her. Don't worry. She'll be fine. I promise." He winked before taking her in his arms again. "This might feel a little odd, but trust me. It won't hurt and we can get to the bed part of our talk sooner."

Vera didn't say anything, just laid her head on his chest and closed her eyes. Gathering his power, Lucifer fixed the image of his hotel room in his mind. Once it was there in every minute detail, he began to loosen his hold on his power and they vanished.

There was only a small tingle in his hands when they reappeared in the middle of his suite.

Chapter Ten

"Oh," Vera gasped once he'd let her go. "How did you do that?"

He shrugged, not really interested in discussing his powers or how they worked. What he was more interested in was getting her under him.

"I can dissolve our bodies into atoms then reassemble them in a different place in the world as long as I can picture that spot in my mind," he told her absently as he started to strip off his jacket.

"Seriously?" She tilted her head to study him.

"Vera?"

"Yes?"

He reached over to tug on her sleeve. "Could you get naked? It's been almost a century since I've been with you, and I don't think I can wait much longer."

She laughed as she started to get undressed. "So suave there, Luka. Oh, should I call you Lucifer?"

"You can call me whatever you want as long as you're screaming it while I fuck you," he muttered.

Vera snorted. "I could probably mange that."

He got his shirt off before he swept her into his arms. Shuddering, he absorbed the touch of her soft hands on his skin. Then she encircled one of his nipples with her lips before sucking on it. Lucifer thrust his hands in her hair, holding her close because he simply wanted to hang on to her and never let her go.

She moved to his other nipple, adding a little bite, and he moaned. His cock stiffened as hard as it ever had and he ached with need. Before he ended up coming in his pants, he gave her a little push away from him.

"What?" She grinned up at him then winked as she reached for his belt. "Are you feeling a little confined?"

"Vera," he whined, brushing her hands away to tear open his pants. Once he was naked, he quickly stripped her then carried her over to the bed.

Sliding her arms up over his shoulders, she spread her legs and he settled between them. He crushed his lips to hers while he rocked against her, running his shaft up and down her pussy. She shuddered when the head of his cock bumped over her clit.

He took one of her nipples in his mouth, flicking it with his tongue a couple of times before pinching it between his teeth and tugging on it. Vera gripped his head and he grunted when she pulled on his hair slightly.

After teasing her breasts a little longer, he trailed kisses down her stomach to her mound. He revealed her clit then pressed his tongue to it before sucking on the piece of flesh.

"Oh, my God, Luka. I've been waiting for this since we said goodbye on the dock," Vera told him.

Lucifer lifted his head to meet her hazel eyes. "I know. I couldn't fuck anyone after I left you. It was as though my body went to sleep that day and only now is it waking up."

"I've never been in love because it's like my heart has been spoken for and I can't give it away. None of my experiences were mind-blowing enough for me to want to repeat them," Vera informed him.

He liked hearing that. Not the part about her sleeping with other men, but he understood that since she hadn't known she was his. Plus they'd been searching for each other through the decades.

"I can't believe we found each other again," he whispered before dipping his head to slide his tongue inside her.

Vera cried out as he slipped his fingers in beside his tongue. He played with her pussy until she was begging for him to take her. Rearing up, he knelt between her thighs before meeting her gaze.

"Are you sure?"

He snorted at the annoyed look she shot him. She poked his leg and glared. "Get on with it, Luka. I want you to make love to me."

Lucifer nodded before spitting on his palm then he slicked up his shaft. He positioned himself at her opening, met her gaze again as he sank into her. Her body took him in as though it had been waiting forever for him.

When he was buried all the way in, he paused to lean down to brush a kiss over her mouth. She entwined her legs around his waist and her arms around his shoulders. Vera clenched her inner muscles. He took that to mean she was ready for him to move, so he began to stroke in and out of her, going slow to start with.

"God, you feel incredible," he said as he thrust into her tight passage. "It's as though you were made for me."

"Maybe I was," she mumbled as they rocked together.

Lucifer thought their bodies fit so perfectly that he couldn't help moving faster and faster, taking her with more and more power.

"I'm sorry if I hurt you," he apologized as he lost control.

"Yes. Please. Harder. I want to feel you, Luka. I want you as deep inside me as you can get. I don't care about bruises or anything," Vera urged him on.

He wouldn't have been surprised if he found nail marks on his flesh in the morning. Their groans mingled as he pistoned his hips back and forth, driving them both closer and closer to the edge. He wanted Vera to come and he was going to do all he could to get her there.

"Luka," Vera yelled as she climaxed and her trembling caught him up.

He slammed into her before freezing. Throwing his head back, he shouted as he flooded her with his cum. Jerking and shuddering, Lucifer felt as though every drop of seed had been drained from him.

When he could make his muscles move, he climbed out of bed before going to clean up. He made sure to wash Vera as well then joined her in bed. They slipped under the blankets, cuddling in each other's arms.

Lucifer played with Vera's brunette curls, twirling them around his fingers while she traced circles on his chest. Something must have occurred to her because she tensed under his hands.

"What's wrong?"

"You didn't use a condom," she pointed out.

He nodded. "I know. It doesn't matter anymore. You're an angel, so you can't get pregnant. Even if you were human, I wouldn't get you pregnant or sick anyway."

"I remember when we made love in Russia. You would never come inside me because you were concerned about me getting with child." She frowned.

"I couldn't very well tell you that there was nothing to worry about because you were an angel and you wouldn't get pregnant if I spilled inside you."

She grimaced then said, "I guess you're right."

He shifted around so she was on her back and he leaned over her. "You're taking this whole thing rather well. I would think you'd freak out to find out that not only are you an angel, but your lover is Lucifer Daystar, the most infamous of the fallen."

Vera cupped his face and smiled up at him. "I'm still processing the whole thing, but it makes sense to me. I've always had these memories of living a life here in Russia and a mysterious lover I'd known then. I always had the feeling that you were more than just a man I'd fallen in love with all those decades ago."

Lucifer lifted one of his shoulders. "I bet falling in love with the devil wasn't on your radar."

Giggling, Vera nodded. "You're right. I wouldn't believe the devil could fall in love, but since you're not the evil creature people make you out to be, I can believe Luka is a wonderful man who's just been misunderstood all these centuries."

"I appreciate it," he murmured as he leaned down to peck a kiss on Vera's lips.

"Also, I have something that kept turning up in my possession over the years. At first, I couldn't understand how—and why—this kept showing up, but when I came to the Hermitage and saw other examples on display, I knew it had to do with you and my past life."

He had an idea what she was talking about, but he asked, "What was it?"

Vera jumped out of bed to race over to where her purse rested on one of the hotel chairs. She dug through it then crowed in triumph when she held up her phone. He couldn't help chuckling as she dashed back to him. Lucifer pushed up to lean against some pillows as he watched her scroll through her pictures.

"Here it is." She held out her phone to show him.

After taking it from her, he stared down at the photo of a small gold egg. It was the Fabergé egg he'd given her in 1918. He'd taken it from the Alexander Palace one day when he'd gone to check on the tsar and his family after the Bolshevik revolution. He'd snuck in, not wanting anyone to know he'd been there or to cause the Romanovs more trouble.

He'd overheard some of the Bolsheviks discussing what they were going to do with the various jewels, paintings and trinkets that graced the walls and rooms of the Palace. Lucifer had known what he did was just as wrong as what the Soviets were going to do, but he couldn't stand the thought that they might get destroyed.

By the time he'd found them again, the royal family had been assassinated and Lucifer had been stunned. Sure, he'd gone through millennia watching mortals kill each other for no other reason than fear, but he'd thought they'd be safe. He'd spent time after their murders trying to help get other members of the Romanov family out of Russia for no other reason than to try and assuage his guilt for not being there to keep them alive.

"I didn't get to them in time," he murmured, running his finger over the screen of the phone.

"I know. I heard about their death before I died from the Spanish Influenza." She rested her hand on his arm. "It wasn't your fault. They were already gone."

"Some would say I did cause them to be killed. That as Lucifer, all the evil in the world rests on my shoulders."

Why was he talking about it? Vera had never seemed to react to the darkness he thought haunted him. He'd always used her acceptance of him to keep him from going over the edge into the insanity that had claimed so many of his fellow fallen.

Vera laughed. "I'm sure you're scary to many of those who fell with you and to the mortals who were supposed to fear you, but I've never truly feared you. You always made me feel safe." She trailed her finger over the slope of his nose. "You still do."

He pulled her down into his arms and he settled into a quiet contemplation of what finding Vera again would mean for him. Lucifer didn't want to continue being the creature everyone feared. He wanted to spend his time with her, loving her until he forgot about the loneliness he'd felt for the years he'd been on earth.

Lucifer slowly drifted to sleep, willing himself to relax for the first time since he'd last held Vera in his arms.

* * * *

A weird thumping intruded on Vera's dreams and she prized her eyes open to find the source of noise. She squeaked in amazement when she found herself sitting on a white couch in a pristine white office.

There was a large mahogany desk in front of her and a man sat behind it.

He finished stapling some papers together, and she recognized it as the thumping that had woken her. When he glanced up to smile at her, she realized she knew him.

"You're Mika'il, Lucifer's friend," she said.

After standing, Mika'il made his way around the desk to prop his butt against the edge of it. He folded his arms over his chest while crossing his legs at the ankles. It was a very relaxed pose and one she found kind of strange for a man wearing a designer suit.

"We used to be best friends, as close as brothers until the fall. Once he chose to rebel against God, I had issues with him."

"I can see where what he did could cause friction between the two of you." Looking around, she noticed how plain the room was. There were two windows, one on each side of the desk, plus a door on the opposite wall. "Where am I?"

"You're in the Waiting Room," Mika'il answered her.

"*The* Waiting Room? What is that exactly?"

Mika'il examined his fingernails. "It's where souls come to decide where they want to spend eternity. Most don't hang around long. Those are the ones who've made up their minds long before they died."

"Holy cow! Am I dead?" She shot to her feet. "I can't be dead. I just found Luka again. Well, I guess he's Lucifer, not Luka, but I have to be able to spend time with him. This isn't fair."

Mika'il held up his hands. "Whoa. Calm down, Vera. You aren't dead. I was just explaining what this place is."

She glared at him. "If I'm not dead, then why am I here?"

"Well, you're here because the Father requested you be at this meeting." Mika'il cleared his throat. "In fact, God requested that you all be here."

"You all?" She eyed the archangel as though she thought he was crazy. "There's only me."

"Actually, it isn't just you anymore," a voice spoke directly behind her.

Vera screamed as she whirled around. There were thirteen other people standing in the room with her. They were paired off, so she knew which guy was with which girl, though there was an extra blond. The said woman strolled over to where Mika'il was and kissed him.

"Why are we here?" the tall blond man asked Mika'il.

"Please, who are all these people and where the hell did they come from?" Vera clasped her hands together.

"These are the seven other lost angels, plus the fallen they've been paired with. Oh and me." Mika'il rubbed his thumb over his woman's bottom lip. "Vera Turnick, this is Celeste and Adam Montgomery. William and Abby Bradford. Dominic and Teresa La Fontaine. Grant and Danielle Carson. Christian and Joan Vosberg. Nevan and Cassandra Largent. This is my beautiful other half, Bridget."

Her head spun from all the names, though she had a vague idea who belonged to what name. "Are you telling me that they are all angels?"

"Celeste, William, Dominic, Danielle, Christian and Cassandra are all fallen angels. You, along with Adam, Abby, Teresa, Grant, Joan, Nevan and Bridget are angels who got misplaced somehow. By pairing us together, it redeemed the fallen while bringing the lost back into the fold." Mika'il rolled his eyes. "It's a long, complicated story and I'm sure your head is spinning from all the names and everything."

"This is only a little confusing," she admitted. "Where is Lucifer? Why am I here, but he isn't?"

"Oh, he'll get here in a second. He hasn't been in this place since his wings were removed, so it might take him a few minutes to find his way back." Mika'il grinned as the door slammed open. "Ah, here he is."

"What the hell are you doing, Mika'il? Are you kidnapping angels now?" Lucifer stalked across the room, ignoring all the others to get to Vera. Once she was in his arms, he looked around and sneered. "Well, if it isn't old home week. I didn't know we were having a reunion. Hope you're not expecting me to re-enact the whole fall. I have no interest in rehashing old news."

Vera saw how Lucifer's presence affected the others. They were tense, watching him as though he were a wild animal waiting to attack at the smallest threat. She stroked her hands up and down his back.

"I'm fine, love. Mika'il said something about us all being here for a meeting. We all kind of kept interrupting him while he was trying to explain." She nuzzled against Lucifer's rigid jaw. "We'll be all right."

"I don't want to be here, Mika'il. This brings back really bad memories for me and I have no wish to kneel before you again." Lucifer snarled, but Vera could see the fear and hurt buried deep in his dark eyes.

"Then you will kneel before me," a resounding voice filled the room and everyone dropped to their knees like it commanded.

A bright light blinded her for a moment and when she blinked to clear her vision, a distinguished older man stood in front of them. He wore a black suit, designer just like Mika'il's, and a white dress shirt. There was an air of total control and supreme confidence surrounding him.

"Father," Mika'il spoke the name with reverence and joy in his voice.

"My dear archangel, you make me proud with every soul you save and demon you defeat. In fact," God said as he gazed upon them, "you all have made me proud."

"Even me?" Lucifer's voice sounded small and uncertain.

Vera found all the air left her lungs when God approached her and Lucifer. He rested his hand gently on the top of Lucifer's golden hair.

"You especially, my beloved angel. You had the hardest job. There were times when I worried that I had asked too much of you, but you proved I was right in trusting you with this most important mission."

"What are you talking about? What mission?" Mika'il asked. He was the only one, aside from Lucifer, who seemed to have regained his ability to speak. The others stared at God in awe.

God went to Mika'il's desk then sat behind it. "Please. Rise all of you. There is no reason for you to kneel before me right now."

"But you're God," Vera pointed out as though no one else had figured it out.

"Yes, I am, Vera, but right now, I must tell you a story and I don't want to do that to the tops of your heads. Take your seats and I'll see if I can clear up some confusion."

There was a frenzied rush as all the angels and fallen found seats then turned their gazes on God as though they were expectant schoolchildren, waiting to hear their morning lessons.

"Each couple here has a story of you, Lucifer. You snuck around, helping them when they didn't even know it was you. You knew about the lost angels and, along with Mika'il, you did your best to make sure these fallen and the lost ones found each other." God smiled and it was as though the sun shined down on Vera's face. "You actively intervened in Joan, Cassandra and Bridget's lives to ensure they were safe until the perfect angel came to them."

Lucifer shrugged. "I was miserable, Father. There was no reason why others should have suffered because of me."

"They didn't suffer because of you, Lucifer. They suffered because of their own arrogance and willingness to be talked into something they knew was wrong." God stopped and tilted his head to one side. "But in the end, none of that matters. What's important is that you've accomplished your mission."

"What mission?" Mika'il stared from God to Lucifer.

God steepled his fingers then tapped them against his chin. "Millennia ago, I approached Daystar and asked him to do something for me. I was worried that mortals were turning away from me. They no longer worshiped me like they had. I thought they needed a being or a figure that would frighten them enough to have them turn back to me."

It was as though a light bulb went on in Vera's head. "You were the reason Lucifer rebelled. You asked him to do it, and being the obedient angel, he did as you asked."

"Yes, and it worked beyond my wildest dreams." God beamed with happiness. "Because of your presence, people continue to worship me and saving their souls is much easier than having to sacrifice my son or destroy the world every time."

"Are you telling me you're the reason Lucifer has been despised all these centuries? Because of some scheme you cooked up?" Vera gritted her teeth at the thought of how hurt Lucifer had been when all his friends had turned their backs on him.

"Vera, shut up. I chose to do it. He didn't force me to fall," Lucifer muttered to her.

"No, Lucifer. She's right to be angry. I shouldn't have asked you to do that without being willing to explain my actions to the others. Yet I guess I was curious to see how many others would follow you without knowing it was all an elaborate ruse." God shrugged. "I found out what I wanted to know."

She reached out to take Lucifer's hand. "It's still not fair."

God's gaze caressed her face and she could feel his love flow over her. "You're right, Vera. It wasn't fair, and I'm going to rectify my actions. All of my lost angels are living in mortal bodies at the moment. When the time comes and these fragile human shells are ready to return to the dust that made them, you will come back to Heaven and take your rightful places."

"Thank you, Father," Bridget spoke from where she sat next to Mika'il. "Your welcome is overwhelming."

"As for the fallen who love you, each of you has sacrificed something for the person you love. You willingly gave your lives, yours souls and your power to keep them safe. You have earned your wings back and your places will be available to you in Heaven.

You will return with your mortal partners when the time comes."

Vera was happy for all the strangers in the room with them, but she didn't really care about them. She wanted to know what would happen to Lucifer when she died and went back to Heaven. She didn't want to be there if he wasn't.

"What about Lucifer?" she asked.

"I don't need anything, Father. Just knowing Vera and the others will be safe where they should have always been is enough for me." Lucifer gripped her hand as though he was begging her not to say anything else.

"I won't be coming back if he's not allowed to return," she stated, not caring that she shouldn't be making demands of God.

God nodded. "I wouldn't have expected anything different from you, Vera, but don't worry. Lucifer has served his purpose well, and mortals no longer need his actual presence to scare them. They have legends and stories to do that. No, when you die and come home, Lucifer is more than welcome to join you here in Heaven."

Lucifer's jaw dropped open then he swallowed. "Are you serious, Father? I can come home?"

"Yes." God looked at each couple then rested his gaze back on Vera and Lucifer. "All of you have learnt the most important lesson of all. You all gave up something for love and that is all I ever really wanted you to know. How to love someone so much, you'd die for them."

Vera looked at Lucifer and knew that even though their journey had never gotten that deadly for either of them, she would have thrown herself in front of a bullet for him. Or have given up her place in Heaven to be with him every minute of the day.

Who knew loving Lucifer would be the wisest thing she'd ever done?

In a blink of her eye, God was gone and they sat stunned, staring at each other. Mika'il looked so guilty. Vera looked at the archangel, surprised by the tears in his silver eyes.

"You mean you weren't responsible for any of it? It was the Father's idea all along," he said to Lucifer who nodded. "I treated you terribly and didn't listen to anything you tried to tell me. I'm so sorry."

Lucifer stood before going over to where Mika'il sat. He held out his hand and Vera held her breath, hoping Mika'il wouldn't turn him away. The archangel jumped to his feet then threw his arms around Lucifer, hugging him close.

She watched as the other fallen and their spouses joined in the welcoming of Lucifer back into the fold. Then Lucifer reached out for her, and she went to him, knowing that he would always look for her to save him from himself.

Epilogue

Sixty years later

Lucifer stared around the Waiting Room, excitement and fear dashing through him. It was the third time he'd been in Mika'il's office.

The first time had been the worst moments of his long eternal life. He'd lost his wings and his home while kneeling in front of Mika'il. His shoulders still burned with pain from Mika'il cutting them from his body. His cheek still ached from the cross-shape brand that had sizzled into his flesh, marking him as the worst of the fallen angels.

He closed his eyes, taking a deep breath as anxiety raced through him. He found himself worried that Mika'il would show up to bar the door leading back into Heaven. It wasn't going to happen. God himself had said Lucifer was welcome to return to their home when Vera's mortal life was over.

He turned to look at the woman he loved. She stood close to him, dressed in white and glowing with happiness. Vera placed her hand on his arm, gesturing toward Mika'il with the other.

"Are you going to say anything to him?"

Lucifer licked his lips and cleared his throat. "I'm not sure I know what to say. I know what the Father said, but there's a small piece of my heart that thinks all of this is a joke. That someone who still hates me is being cruel to make me think that Heaven is open to me again."

Mika'il sighed. "I would never do that to you, Lucifer. I've gone over and over everything you've ever said to me, and I realize you've been dropping hints about what had really happened since the beginning. I was too proud and too hurt to listen to you."

"Hurt?"

"You were my best friend. The one person who I thought I knew better than anyone else. Only God was more important in my eyes. Suddenly you're rebelling against the Father, demanding to be treated as higher in God's heart than the mortals he created." Mika'il shrugged. "I didn't know how I could've missed the fact that you were crazy."

Vera laughed and Lucifer smiled.

"That is true. Anyone who truly thought God would love anyone more than he does mortals had to be crazy," he admitted. "It's not your fault that you didn't believe me. I had to make it realistic."

"You did a good job." Mika'il motioned for Lucifer and Vera to come closer to the door. When they did, the archangel said, "The others have already returned and have gone on to be welcomed back into Heaven. You two are the last ones."

"What will happen now?" he couldn't help but ask.

"What do you mean?" Mika'il frowned.

"To the mortals. Without me around to fear, they won't have a reason to pray to God for salvation or protection." Lucifer entwined his fingers with Vera, not wanting to go back to earth, but wondering if his leaving was a good idea.

"There are legends and myths built around your presence. It's almost as though they've taken on a life of their own. Just the memory of you will be enough to bring people to their knees and have them begging for God's forgiveness." Mika'il slapped Lucifer on his shoulder. "You did your job well, my friend."

Lucifer exhaled sharply. "Never let it be said that I was lazy, or anything like that."

Mika'il pointed to the door. "Are you ready?"

"Not in the least," he muttered but took a step toward it.

Vera squeezed his hand. "I'm right here with you. We'll go through together."

He glanced over at her and gasped. White feathered wings rose from her back to flutter around her. Then there was a slight tug at his shoulders and a familiar heaviness there. After flexing his shoulders, a gentle breeze washed over his ears. His hand shook as he reached back to touch his wings. Tears filled his eyes.

"I never thought I'd ever have these back," he confessed while wiping his wet cheeks dry.

"You can't be an angel without wings," Mika'il reminded him. "Now go on through. There are people waiting to greet you."

Lucifer straightened his back, enjoying the sensation of his wings wafting behind him as he approached the door. He didn't let go of Vera though, taking a hold of the doorknob with his free hand.

Closing his eyes, Lucifer watched as all the long, solitary years of his life flashed by him. All the times when he had done terrible things because it had been expected of him or because no one had thought he would do anything else. Times when he'd helped mortals simply because it had made him feel better, not because he'd thought it would earn him a gold star on a board somewhere in Heaven.

He saw Joan, Cassandra and Bridget. Three lost and fallen angels who he'd watched over until their destined partners had appeared. It had been hard to be there when each of them had fallen in love and found their way home to Heaven, especially to see Bridget and Mika'il discover and give their hearts to each other.

Lucifer had come to the conclusion that day that he was never meant to be anything other than a pawn in a game God was playing with the mortals. He wasn't going to find Vera again—that he'd lost his one chance at love when he'd lost her in 1918. It had been a painful lesson to learn, but he'd done his best to accept it.

"Are you ready?" Vera's question was soft.

"Thank you for loving me when you didn't know who I was, and for not turning away from me when you found out the truth." He kissed her. "You were the one who gave me strength to remain focused on my job, and not fall into the abyss so many of my brethren have lost themselves in."

Vera kissed him back. "Thank you for finding me, even when I didn't realize I was lost. You gave me back my place in a world I can't wait to see."

"We're returning together and in the end, that's all that matters. Love is the whole reason this adventure began."

"And it's the reason why it's ending." Vera's love for him shined in her eyes, and Lucifer knew he would never doubt her feelings for him.

He opened the door, breathing deeply of the clean, fresh air drifting through the entranceway. Blue skies and golden sunlight greeted his eyes. Warmth touched his skin and soul, making him acknowledge that there had always been a piece of his heart encased in ice from the moment he'd been banished. He could feel it thawing as they stepped over the threshold, through the gate, and into Heaven where hundreds of angels gathered, waiting to welcome him back to the only place he would ever call home.

Vera's laugh drew his attention, and he amended his oath. Wherever Vera was the only place he'd consider home. That place being Heaven was a bonus.

God's voice danced in his mind and brushed against his heart. *"Yet here you are, about to step into the very place you never thought you'd be welcomed again. You proved yourself a loyal and loving servant, Lucifer Daystar. I will always consider your sacrifice worthy of all the joys Heaven can give you."*

About the Author

I've been writing for most of my life, but was first published in 2004. I believe everyone deserves love in all its forms. I write about women and men who find strength in loving each other. I live in the Midwest with my two cats, and when I'm not writing (which isn't very often) I read and watch movies.

Tiffany Aaron loves to hear from readers. You can find her contact information, website details and author profile page at http://www.totallybound.com.

Totally Bound Publishing